A

THOUSAND

GRACES

for John

with my best wishes

[signature]

Senyume Press

ISBN: 979-8-218-10984-4

A THOUSAND GRACES

A NOVEL

KAREN HILL ANTON

SENYUME PRESS

1

There were exactly eleven houses on this road that had no name. Everyone called it Uchida Road because most of the people who lived there bore the name Uchida. There was a connection, an invisible chain that linked the houses because they were *shinseki*, relatives. The link began long ago and was forever complicated by marriage, birth, and death, and in one case, adoption. Now, in 1969, it had all become vague, but still there was connection.

All the way up Uchida Road you could see houses off to the right. Some were set back from the road and built into the mountainside like bird perches, others, right at the road edge. To the left was the river. Cold as ice from early autumn on, the river was the only refuge in the hot, thickly humid summers. The three cold months of winter, people shut themselves up in their houses, hardly leaving their yards. These houses—old farmhouses—weren't cozy. Drafts blew through their cracks, windows were often makeshift, added after the fact. *Nabe*, one-clay-pot meals, were eaten huddled around the *kotatsu*, the charcoal brazier. The people of Uchida Road went straight from the table to the *ofuro*, and straight from that hot soaking bath to their futon. It was how to stay warm. These close mountains kept the winter sun out. It would seem the first people who settled there had chosen the place by mistake.

The surrounding mountains appeared like they'd provide coolness in the hot weather, but they served to trap heat, and no breeze escaped their fastness. In summer, the river was the place to be. The children went down to the river after lunch and stayed until just before dark. The men went whenever they took a break and stood in the water, cooling themselves while fishing for the small tasty *ayu*. Salted and grilled right there by the side of the river, the fish made a good snack. The men gave them to the children, too, and still there were plenty to put in bamboo baskets to take back to family kitchens. When they could, the women went and stood at the water's edge, cooling their feet. Always in their aprons, they went only to watch the children. They never swam.

Chie Uchida's house was the last on that long, winding road. Like the others, she spent every summer day of her childhood at that river. She never ate the fish the men of the village offered and swam away from their small smokey fires. Her mother, too, would come and stand.

"Mother, do you know how to swim?" Chie would ask. Of course, her mother answered, every time. But Chie never asked her why she didn't go in the water. Naturally, her mother also had on her apron. It was impossible to imagine her in a bathing suit, impossible to imagine her enjoying the freedom of floating in the water. Chie wanted to tell her mother how good it felt to let the small, cooling waves lap over her body as they brushed her to the river's edge.

·   ·   ·

Chie was taller than everyone in her family. A too-tall girl was not considered a good thing, and she'd only recently stopped hunching her shoulders after realizing it was useless trying to take centimeters off her height. Still, she was self-conscious that she was taller than her brother, Isao. With short, sturdy legs under a body that was perfectly square, he'd come in the world built for farm work, or so it appeared. They hardly looked like siblings. Chie and Isao both had a clear memory of another sibling, their brother Minoru, born between them. He had died July 3, 1959, ten years earlier, the day after his fifth birthday. Because it had been a *Fuun no hi*, a bad luck day, he was never talked about, and it was as though he'd never existed. But Chie could still see his misshapen head, bony legs and arms. She could still feel how his skin felt to the touch, like paper, and that it was always the color of hers when she was very cold.

Chie was aware her small voice didn't match her height. Her clear brown eyes, a shade lighter than anyone might expect, were always the cause for a second look. With her willowy limbs she looked out of place among the farming people, often short and stout, or short and thin. Her mother told Chie she'd wanted to name her Yuri for her favorite flower, Lily. Mr. Uchida's father, given the honor, named her Chie. A thousand graces.

No school today. It was Sunday. The slight breeze Chie felt as she sat at her desk was just cool enough to let her know it wasn't spring yet, but that spring was the next season, and it was on its way.

"Chie. Bring me my bonnet, will you?" Her mother stood at the entranceway to the large farmhouse, facing the stairs so her voice would carry and she wouldn't need to unfasten her work shoes to enter.

"Yes, Mother," Chie answered, making her small voice loud. She came downstairs and took the bonnet off the hook in the kitchen where her mother always hung it when she came in from the fields to prepare meals.

"What are you doing?"

"Homework." Chie put the pencil she held in her right hand into her pocket and handed her mother the bonnet. "I'll be finished soon. I'll come and help."

It was tea-picking time, and it all had to be done in a few days—picking, drying, and packaging. When her mother was a schoolgirl, the children were let out to pick tea and to plant and harvest rice. *Mikan* too. These mandarin oranges grew in great abundance in their region. Now children were let out when they had a big test coming up.

"No, no. You finish your schoolwork."

After Chie's grandmother, her father's mother, died, Chie's mother had taken over all the farm work, as if the two of them hadn't been doing it together right up to the moment the old woman lay down on cool tatami and closed her eyes for the last time. The day when Chie came in from school and saw her grandmother lying there, Chie knew she was dead. The very old woman always lay down on the tatami to nap. No pillow, she'd curl up like a cat, her arm bent to support her head. That day Chie found her stretched out, her arms and legs as straight as a soldier's.

Chie went back upstairs to her room. The second story of the old farmhouse had been used only for storage, but the day Chie got her period, her mother said Chie and her brother had to stop sharing a room. Working without stopping, her mother cleared away all the stored chests and boxes, simply making them disappear. Chie had always wondered, though only vaguely, what could be in those chests.

"Oh, nothing. Just old stuff that should probably be thrown out," her mother, knowing she would never throw it out, had said when Chie asked. Deciding to look for herself, Chie had lifted the black wooden lid on a chest that originally was used to store tea. She found layers of kimono and obi, sashes. Old, the colors dull and faded, these were nothing like the kimono printed with bright butterflies and flowers, obi woven with intricate patterns, she saw in magazines and shop windows. Her mother was right. They should be thrown out. There was no treasure here.

Chie sat at her desk, reminded again of how much she wished her mother hadn't bought the desk. The money could have been used for more useful things, but every event in Chie's life was, for her mother, a chance to do something, to make or buy something. It was how her mother showed caring, and her whole life was spurred on by these occasions that marked passing or changing: entering school, learning to swim, being selected for the chorus, menstruation. It didn't matter—it could be anything that marked a change.

Chie didn't need a day off to study for a test. Maybe the rest of the school did. She was a good student, practically embarrassed by her *seiseki*, class standing. It wouldn't win her friends. She knew her teachers would soon begin to encourage her to go to college. And then her problems would begin because she would be presented with the world of possibilities.

Chie had gone on to high school watching more than half of

her class leave ninth grade and leave schooling for the last time of their fifteen-year-old lives. They were now working at home on family farms. Some of the girls might work in shops as cashiers. The boys could work as junior auto mechanics. In a few years they'd all be married. Children would follow, and life would be a settled matter. So simple. So uncomplicated. So what she didn't want.

Marriage and children would be all right with her, one day. But she didn't want that day to come too soon, before she was ready, before she had seen or done anything that wasn't prede-termined. She wondered how much of her life she would be able to create, how much she would be able to leave up to chance. While she sensed the temptation of what could be imagined, she was fearful of what was unknown, and feared most any big change that would take her away from her life, her family, from all she knew. Still, she could spend hours daydreaming about things she knew she didn't know. She wanted to know so much more about history, geography, biology —much more than she learned in school. She kept her interest in English to herself. She felt English, especially, would get her in trouble. She had found out too much through reading, found there was a world available to her, through books, that was not meant to be there for her. Reading could have no more purpose than to make her curious about a life she could never know. But she realized she could know it. Because it existed, it also existed for her. And it made her a dreamer. Waking up from a night's sleep, quiet and alone, she would dream while fully awake.

"Chie, let's meet after school on Saturday," her friend Kimiko said.

"But we have chorus practice."

"I know. But we'll be finished by three o'clock. Four at the latest."

"But what about homework?"

"Oh, I'm going to do it on Sunday. That'll be plenty of time. Come on. Let's meet."

Standing in the entrance of her house, Chie talked into the telephone. It was still early and cold and she could see the kotatsu from where she stood. The thought ran through her mind that if the phone were inside, she could sit at the kotatsu and be comfortable and warm while she talked. But she was sure there had been no question about where the telephone should go when it had been put in. Like every other house on Uchida Road, the telephone, placed on a cushion to soften the ring, sat on a small table facing the *genkan*, entranceway.

"Okay. But I'll have to see if there's anything I need to do at home first." Even as Chie spoke, she knew there was always something that needed to be done at home, though her mother was intent on making it appear that nothing was ever needed, and if it were, she could do it herself.

Since she was a small girl, Chie felt she had seen her mother's face divided into the upper and lower halves. The lower half showed her mouth relaxed in a soft smile, covering teeth that weren't good, but were well taken care of—a toothpick employed after every meal meant her gums glowed a deep healthy pink. The eyes of the upper half seemed like they didn't belong to the face below them. And it wasn't just the eyes. The skin around them was worn, worn out. Those eyes revealed everything and had no connection to the smile below.

Her mother would get dressed up just to go shopping, which was as much of a social occasion as she ever participated in. The clothes she wore, bought in local stores with poor lighting and little stock, made her look forlorn. These were the shops that clothed local women in a palette of gray, brown, tan, and shades of mauve nowhere else to be seen on the planet. Colors that came with the expectation that these women fade into their places, in the background. Her mother did on occasion don a favorite pink blouse with lace around a high collar. The color, next to her face plastered with low-priced pancake makeup encrusted in the lines around her mouth and eyes, made her look garish, even ghoulish. Her usual farm work outfits of cotton pants and shirts with traditional prints always covered by an apron or smock were much more fitting.

When Chie's mother's elder sister married, the husband came into the house. He was adopted into their family, *engumi*, as was the custom when there is no son. He took the family's name and took over. Chie's mother, Tsuya, the youngest of four sisters, was still at home and remembered that from the moment the wedding sake was drunk, it was clear he had accepted and assumed the role of master of the house.

Her mother's two eldest sisters had been killed in a bus accident. They were seventeen and eighteen years old. It was their first trip on a bus. Chie often wondered if it had been because of the death of these two beloved sisters that her mother had tried to fill the blanks in her own mother's life. Chie knew, or she'd heard, her grandmother would not eat for a week after the deaths of her first two daughters. Her family had to force her to drink water, and finally she did, saying she could not produce more tears without it. "I am a woman cursed to live forever wretched after her children are dead. Who will weep for me?"

Chie's mother would. She wept and resolved to give her life in futile attempt to replace the two lost daughters. She quit school with her mother's blessing, though her elder sister tried to get her to continue. Tsuya practically never left her mother's side. She married the first man her mother suggested and responded to her mother's request "give me children" by giving birth to a daughter, her mother's first grandchild. The woman lived to see her second grandchild, the grandson Minoru, enter kindergarten. But not long enough to know he would be dead before elementary school.

"You're late."

"Yes, I know. I missed the first train and had to wait fifteen minutes," Chie said, knowing Kimiko knew exactly how much time was needed to wait between trains.

"You didn't really want to come," Kimiko said, sticking out one of her beautiful legs as her hand rested on the hip of her short forest green skirt. As usual, she was dressed perfectly for the occasion: Saturday afternoon casual. Stockings with a slight dark green tint covered legs that were athletic from doing nothing whatsoever, and her small feet were tucked into a pair of black leather shoes with a dark green leather bow. Where did she find these things? How did she always get them to match? In the same moment, Chie was hopelessly aware of her own shoes, worn out and worn down at the heels. Her incongruously large feet didn't appear to match her lithesome body. When she found a pair of shoes that fit, she had to wear them until she could find another pair. And when it came to makeup, Kimiko somehow managed to wear it without it being the least bit noticeable, while if Chie wore even the lightest makeup, the emphasized color made her look tawdry. Expertly applied following the instructions in the many women's magazines Kimiko read, her rosy lipstick gave her mouth a pretty pout.

"You didn't really want to come," she repeated.

"That's not true. I did. I'm here, aren't I?" Chie said, aware that was a ridiculous defense.

"Did you bring money?" Kimiko asked, letting Chie know by her question that whatever she brought it wouldn't be enough.

"Of course."

Kimiko and Chie were closest friends. Or oldest friends. Or they knew each other longer than they knew anyone else. They were, in fact, related, though neither of them could ever remember, or cared, how. The concept of friends didn't carry any meaning for either of them. It just meant they spent a lot of their free time together, that they exchanged manga. Kimiko didn't like reading and firmly resisted when Chie tried to turn their exchanges into novels. They knew each other's favorite foods and colors, but there was no talk, or even expectations, of loyalty, or any other features thought to denote friendship. They were just friends.

Kimiko had everything, or at least everything that Chie sometimes thought she wanted. Kimiko's parents had recently rebuilt their house, taking their old farmhouse down to its foundation and replacing it in record time with a structure of plasticized wood and aluminum siding. Their house was the first one in view when entering Uchida Road, and there seemed to be a general feeling that they should be at the forefront of all change, of new ways of doing things. No one was surprised when the large woodpile, which was used to heat the bath and could be seen from the road, did not reappear when the new house was completed. From now on, they would be heating the bath with gas, and from now on, all the people on Uchida Road knew what they must strive for: a gas-heated bath. Five years from now, ten years, it didn't matter. It was just important that this was one of the new things to be acquired.

Kimiko, an only child, had those things that children without siblings could get. Her own room. Not a leftover storage space like Chie's, nor what their schoolmates endured—tatami rooms, shared with their mothers, without walls but with sliding doors that opened onto other rooms. Kimiko's room was constructed especially for her, with her in mind. Decorated with ideas from the pages of a teen magazine, her room boasted a bed, maybe the only one on Uchida Road. There was a stand-alone closet and a chest of drawers that matched the small night table. Curtains—not *shoji*, rice paper screens—covering the windows carried out the red-and-white color theme that touched everything. And she had a telephone. No other kid in their school had a telephone in their room.

Kimiko had more clothes than she'd ever be able to wear. It wasn't possible—they wore school uniforms six days a week most days of the year. While Chie's feet seemed to gain a few centimeters with every year, Kimiko's small feet had stopped growing years earlier, and even the large new shoe cabinet in the entranceway could hardly hold the shoes she constantly bought. Her only-child status kept her in money. Besides the bounty she came into when she collected *otoshidama*, the New Year's gift money, her parents seemed to have no idea what amount of money was necessary, or appropriate, for the allowance of a seventeen-year-old.

"I thought first we'd go to the movies and then perhaps have lunch later," Kimiko said as they walked toward the movie house. Kimiko made these odd stabs at speaking in polite language, and nothing could have been more out of character. She could have said what she meant: "We'll go to the movies and then have lunch."

"Sure," Chie said, unsuccessfully trying to hide the fact that she doubted whether she had the money for the movies, lunch, and the train ticket home.

"The movie is my treat," Kimiko said.

"Really?" Chie said. "Is it all right?" This was one of the few instances it could be all right—Kimiko was a relation. "Thanks."

The theater was full of other high school girls—all in various getups, indulging in the forbidden pleasure of not wearing their uniforms, which they were supposed to wear whether in school or not. And every one of them was breaking the school's strict rule: *One may attend the cinema only in the company of one's parents.*

Chie could not have survived watching this movie in the company of her parents. And even being with Kimiko was almost more than Chie could bear. She'd seen movies in which the lovemaking had appeared real, but it was as if the director winked to let you know it was all make-believe. But there was no wink this time. This simulation was much too real. Chie realized she was seeing, was involved in, people making love, having sex, for the first time. Mercifully, no one could see her face. She could feel the flush. She was not shocked. She was interested. Aroused by the possibilities of sex, she wished she could see the scene over and over. She could sense Kimiko intently reading the subtitles that ran vertically on the right side of the picture.

But Chie could follow the language of this young New York couple. And she believed the celluloid man loved the celluloid woman.

"Did you like the movie?" Kimiko asked over the phone that evening.

What did she want to hear? Yes would mean Chie liked the sex scenes. "I thought it was interesting," she said.

"Yeah, but did you like it?" Kimiko asked again, from the comfort and privacy of her room.

Chie's eyes could not even meet her mother's as the woman glanced up from the low table where the family now sat eating.

"I thought it was good."

"But did you like it?" Kimiko said again, insistent.

"Look. I've got to go. We're starting dinner. I'll see you at school."

She wasn't hungry. They'd had a big lunch, which Kimiko paid for. Chie hadn't eaten much from the buffet, though Kimiko had encouraged her: "This place is great! You can eat as much as you like! Stop being so careful. Pile it on your plate!"

"What's the matter?" Chie's mother asked. "Why aren't you eating? Don't you feel well? Do you have a fever?"

"No, Mother, I'm fine. Just not very hungry."

Her mother ate copious amounts, always. And always solicitous, and a little worried, she could not countenance Chie missing, or not eagerly eating, a meal.

"Take a bath, and get in bed," her mother said to Chie's back as Chie excused herself from the table. "I'll bring you some hot water with *umeboshi*, pickled plum."

. . .

Chie looked at herself in the mirror of the little dressing area adjoining the bath. Her skin, still releasing steam, showed the deep rose color she knew her face had been at the movies. Looking at her body, she saw it was so unlike her mother's short, flat frame. Indeed, it was like the woman's in the movie. Smooth, unblemished skin covered the perfect circles of her small breasts. The narrow hips of her lower body ended in long, strong legs that could have been the legs of a ballet dancer.

"So, what did you think? Huh?" Kimiko had waited at the bottom of the road so they could ride their bicycles to school together.

"Good morning," Chie said. Kimiko didn't usually wait when Chie was late, and she was late today. "Think about what?"

"About the movie!"

Before she'd gone to sleep last night, Chie promised herself that no amount of wheedling from Kimiko was going to get Chie to discuss that movie—which would mean discussing sex. She wasn't going to share her feelings or her thoughts with Kimiko.

"Oh, I've already forgotten the movie. We've got a big test today. Did you study?"

"Oh, forget the test," Kimiko said as they peddled uphill and she could no longer use her breath for talking. Though she managed to say, " 'Forgotten.' Liar."

2

During the last year of high school and from the year before, Chie's teachers made a concerted effort to get her to apply to a four-year college. But the effort was far from in concert as each teacher wanted to take the credit for guiding the school's star student. It was Chie herself who'd been exemplary in practically teaching herself English. Listening and practicing with cassette tapes, she was diligent in following the regularly broadcast English lessons on public broadcasting radio and television. Very few students from the school went on to four-year universities, and certainly no girls. The two-year colleges were considered good enough, really, indeed a fine finish to a girl's education. At her graduation, Chie said goodbye to classmates she knew she'd never see again, though she knew their fate.

There was no question that Chie would pass the test for the junior college. Although it was considered the best one in the area, it was hardly more than a preparatory school for the office staff the young women would become before they became wives. This was most evident in that Kimiko, with her poor grades, had also been accepted to the same school. There was something ludicrous about Kimiko and Chie attending the same institution of higher learning. Chie was in the department of English. Kimiko went into the commerce department, the department that trained young women in the skills needed to be "office ladies." Having a junior college diploma under her belt, just like her much-touted piano lessons, and the additional sure knowledge her parents would pay for a fine wedding, assured her a good marriage—to a company man, not a farmer. Kimiko had little else on her mind than marriage.

Kimiko's parents paid the exorbitant deposit money for an apartment near the college, and for half the monthly rent, Chie could have lived with her, but she preferred to commute. Or rather, she preferred not to live with Kimiko, and knew that her help could be used at home.

Isao had gone off to live and work on their aunt's farm. Although he'd probably learn little of practical value since the farm, in the northern province of Aomori, produced apples, his parents thought that because it was a large operation, he'd be learning valuable know-how that might help turn their small tea and mikan production into a financially secure, if modest, business. While it was still expected that Chie, as the eldest daughter, might marry and her husband be adopted into her family, Isao and Chie, between themselves, had already agreed he would be the one to stay on in the family home.

Chie and Isao were close like sisters. They'd shared a room growing up, and shared the knowledge of the lost brother, Minoru, whose name was never mentioned in the house. It was as if Minoru was a secret. The worst thing about Chie getting her own room was not being able to fall asleep while talking to Isao. Since they were very young, she'd tell him stories in the dark. At first, she made them up based on storybooks, and later they followed themes from books she read, the main characters replaced with herself and Isao. Chie went deep into her imagination to make up exciting tales for Isao. No matter how sleepy he was, he'd fight to keep his eyes open. Sometimes there would be long pauses while she thought something up and figured out how to change the story to relate to them and their life. Isao seemed to be holding his breath, and Chie would think he'd fallen asleep, but she'd never check, never break the precious spell her stories wove around them in the darkened room that always smelled like damp wood. She'd wait until she heard his nearly imperceptible soft breathing that told her he was asleep, and then she could sleep too.

When she wasn't daydreaming, telling stories and reading stories were Chie's happiest moments. During those young years in the darkened room, she hadn't yet dreamed that one day she'd be asked to read, and it would take up and represent the best part of her day.

In this class we will look at fiction
from the viewpoint of modern women writers, examining
their impact on contemporary society.

Chie had to read the seminar description in the brochure several times. Although she understood it, there was something unusual about the language: it showed expectation. It was clear this course would be more demanding than her high school English class, which asked no more of her than to memorize vocabulary, summarize short passages, and adhere strictly to rules of grammar. And this class bore no resemblance at all to her first introduction to English in junior high school, where English was presented as though it were an esoteric, arcane, and dead language, hardly the international language of the century they were living in.

She flipped to the faculty biographies. *Carl Rosen, Associate Professor of English. Bachelor of Arts, State University of New York at Binghamton; Master of Arts, Columbia University, New York City; Master of Arts in Teaching, School for International Training, Vermont.*

She knew a foreigner taught the English classes, but she couldn't have imagined that the course titled "Women Writers in the Twentieth Century" would be taught by a man—and wondered that this Carl Rosen would know so much about women writers. About women.

Sitting near the door at the far end of the room, with about ten young women gathered around a conference table, Chie listened intently as Carl Rosen intoned, "I will try to speak slowly and clearly, but if there is anything you don't understand, please stop me."

It couldn't be possible, Chie thought to herself, that he could really believe that any of these young women would stop a teacher, a man, in midsentence.

"Of course, we will do plenty of listening practice in the language laboratory, and we will focus on conversational speaking in my Oral English class. I hope to see some of you in those classes as well."

Chie found herself pondering what kind of foreigner this Rosen-sensei was. She knew he was American, but she'd never seen any American men quite like the man who sat at the head of the table in the seminar room. He was not tall, maybe just her height. And he was so dark. Could there be white Americans as dark as this one? She couldn't tell if he were tanned or always this dark. Could New York be so sunny? Although obviously freshly shaven, he had a beard that looked like it couldn't wait to grow out. And he smelled of aftershave. Someone will have to tell him, she thought. It was simply not acceptable for a man, a teacher, a professor, to reek of cologne. The thick dark hair on the back of his hands matched the hair on his head, which had not been touched recently by a barber's scissors. It's possible, Chie thought, that he always wore his hair this long, allowing it to touch the collar of his olive-green suit jacket. Olive green? It was a good match for his skin color, but a teacher in green?

"In Oral English, class sizes will be a bit larger than this seminar," he went on, "but you will also have one-on-one instruction as well as pair practice."

Although all the seminar students were required to take the Oral English classes, Chie wondered if he knew that the last thing most of these young women wanted was "one-on-one" instruction. The basic idea was to get through the two years and get out. And get married.

"We will be reading all these writers over the course of the year," Carl Rosen said as he passed out the reading list. "I had the library order the books, but there will only be one copy of each title. Paperback editions of the books are available through the student bookstore."

Was he American? He didn't talk like anyone she'd ever heard. Although he was supposed to be from New York, he didn't sound at all like the actor who had played in the movie about the young New York City couple. That man had been tall with dark hair, his clear skin looked like he may have never shaved, his light eyes were so blue, so fresh, somehow so American.

Chie glanced down at the list in her hands: *Choose from any of the shorter works of fiction (novels, short stories) of the following authors: Doris Lessing, Iris Murdoch, Toni Morrison, Eudora Welty.*

Chie was baffled. She'd read many books in English, but this list didn't have the names of any of the writers she was familiar with—Agatha Christie, for example, who Chie knew had written something like a hundred books. Chie looked up at the dark professor. Did he really know about women writers?

"Rosen-sensei."

"Yes?"

"I'm Uchida Chie. Excuse me. Chie Uchida."

"Yes." Carl Rosen stood up from his desk. "How do you do?"

"How do you do?" Chie was flustered. This response didn't sound like the right one. What was the right response? She drew a blank, and anyway, it was too late.

"Yes?" Carl Rosen said again.

She told herself to relax, to just speak as she normally did, but to do it in English. And to speak faster before he had a chance to say yes again.

"I have been assigned to assist you. With setting up the class. Arranging the materials in the language laboratory." She felt better now. She had said what she meant. She had pronounced the *l*'s clearly.

"Oh yes." He used his left hand to brush his hair back while offering the right to shake. "Thank you."

A thick lock of hair fell over his eyes, and Chie realized this must be something that happened regularly.

They were the same height, and she looked right into his eyes. What an odd color, she thought to herself. His hazel eyes didn't seem to belong to a face with such dark skin. She'd never seen anyone who was so striking in appearance, features with such sharp contrasts. Although his prominent nose would be described in Japanese as *takai*, there was nothing "tall" about this nose.

"Yes?" she heard him say.

She flushed, realizing she must have been staring at him, or at least keeping her gaze on him too long.

"Oh, yes," she said, and in that moment felt glad she'd worn her new dress. She'd hardly been adventurous in picking it out. Navy blue, it was the color of the uniform she'd worn throughout junior high and high school. Still, it fit her perfectly, and lay on her body like a compliment. Merino wool, it fell over her breasts lightly, just touched the waist, and covered her knees. "When would you like me to come?"

"Yes, let's see." He shuffled some papers on the desk as he glanced at them. "Oral English is Monday and Thursday, from ten thirty. It's ninety minutes. If you come to my office a half hour ahead of time, I could give you the key to the laboratory."

Carl sat down at the desk and, turning to Chie, said, "Even ten fifteen would be fine. I may just need you to make some copies. There isn't much to do."

"Okay. I will come then. Thank you."

"Thank *you*," she heard Carl Rosen say, though she was not sure if he'd emphasized the last word.

3

C hie's mother let her help with the housework and cooking, and light chores like laundry, but she was adamant about not letting her daughter do any work in the fields. She believed it would ruin Chie. Thinking that once she started, once it was known and familiar, her daughter would not be able to break out of the cycle of planting and weeding, tending and harvesting. There would be no escape. Her mother shuddered at the thought of Chie's hands becoming rough and hard, the nails broken across the tops, her back curling, and lines forming around her mouth and eyes too early. That's not what she wanted for her Lily.

Chie now had more time than she could ever remember having before. She had four days of classes, and they didn't add up to five-hour days. The forty-five-minute train ride to and from the college in the city, Takaizu, gave her even more time to do the required reading for the English seminar she had signed up for. This class she knew would be more challenging than the others because she'd be expected not just to read and study, but also to express her opinions. She got on the train, looking forward to losing herself in the Doris Lessing novel *The Grass Is Singing*, when, just as the doors were closing, Kimiko jumped onto the train and fell into the seat next to Chie, bumping her and knocking her book to the floor.

"Whew. I just made it."

"Kimiko," Chie said, picking up her book and sticking it in her bag, "I thought you were riding your motor scooter." She knew Kimiko had been home for the weekend.

"A friend drove me." It wasn't necessary for Kimiko to name or clarify who this friend might be. Chie was sure it must be a boyfriend. "And anyway, I'll be getting rid of that old thing." She primly put her legs together and lined up her feet in rose-pink patent leather shoes. The color perfectly matched the color of the roses that made the pattern on her spring dress. It was still a little cool and when Chie had left the house, she thought her light gray woolen skirt suited the weather, but now she wished that she, too, had worn a spring dress.

"But it's new," Chie said, remembering the day Kimiko rode the shiny purple motor scooter to her house to show her.

"I've started driving lessons," Kimiko said as she arranged her pretty dress neatly around her legs. She was so neat and orderly when it came to her clothes, like she could be polite to clothes but not to people. "They'll buy me a car before summer."

"Wow." Chie didn't even know what a car cost, but she knew driving lessons were expensive. She, too, planned to take driving lessons, but knew she wouldn't be able to afford them anytime soon.

An apartment, a boyfriend, and now a car. It wasn't that

Chie even wanted these things, but she knew what they meant. Independence. Freedom. She could hardly imagine it. Rather, she had only imagined it. The books and stories she read gave her ideas of such things, and in the stories she'd made up for Isao, there was always a boy and a girl without parents. Sometimes they lived in an old house in the mountains, sometimes in an apartment in Tokyo or a beautiful villa in France. It didn't matter. There was this girl and boy who lived freely in this wonderful place, and something exciting was always happening to them.

"Stop by after your class."

"I really should go straight home," Chie said.

"Aw, come on. You haven't even seen my place," Kimiko said as they stepped out of the train. Either she was in a daze, or she really didn't notice she was bumping into people boarding the train. "Stop pretending like you're so busy. I know you don't do any work at home!" Kimiko laughed.

"Well, I guess it would be all right for a short visit. I still must make the train back. Tell me where your apartment is."

Kimiko stopped in her tracks, oblivious to the throng about to board the train, ripped a page from her notebook, and drew a map.

"I don't know if I can find it. I've never been around there before," Chie said, looking at Kimiko's scribbled map.

"Oh, it's easy. It's the first street on the left after you pass Yuzuki," naming the famous *wagashiya*. Well-known for its traditional Japanese sweets, the store had a plaque at its entrance stating proudly that it was established the first year of the Showa era, 1926. Now, with the shop almost fifty years in the same location, the surrounding neighborhood had become upscale. Kimiko mentioning Yuzuki made it clear that she, too, was living in Takaizu's most exclusive neighborhood.

"Okay. See you later then," Chie said as she left Kimiko at the main entrance of the college and they went in separate directions.

The English department had its own new building, attached to the college's library. A modern concrete structure, it was completely incongruous with the other, older college buildings. Those buildings, mostly a pinkish brick, had years of mold and grime collected around the roof, and every rainy season—in this region they could count on a full month of rain—seemed to melt this mixture and send it dripping down from the eaves. These buildings, built in the early fifties after the war, lacking in any architectural distinction, could not even be described as utilitarian. They were not structures any architect would attach his name to. No campus connected them, but rather the six separate buildings that made up the college were spread out through a small, old neighborhood of the city. After crossing the street after the home economics class, students would pass a dentist office and perhaps an old woman walking with a support stroller, before entering the school's gym. The gym itself was old but had been refurbished several times. Now it had, besides a volleyball court, a partitioned area with a floor especially laid for modern dance and stretching exercise. For years the instructor persevered teaching dance classes while volleyballs passed overhead, steadily accompanied by the *pop pop* of ping pong.

Chie came through the first-floor passageway connecting the English department building with the library. Just getting to the passage was like going through a maze, and she emerged in the bare concrete lobby, with its large wooden abstract sculpture in the center. Somehow it made her feel lost. The world of rural southern Africa evoked in the Lessing novel and lingering in her thoughts added to her feeling of being removed from the place she now stood.

"Oh, hello." Suddenly, she heard herself speaking. Carl Rosen stood squarely in front of her.

"Good morning," he said cheerily. "I recognized you." He seemed proud of himself.

"Good morning, Professor Rosen."

"Uchida Chie. Right?"

"That's right."

"Are you on your way to the language lab?"

"Yes. I am just now going there."

"Good. I will walk with you."

As they walked toward the end of the corridor on their way up to the second-floor lab, Carl Rosen said, "So I see you like to read."

"Excuse me?"

"You enjoy reading, don't you? I see you in the library every day."

"Yes. I like reading very much."

"Who are your favorites?"

"Excuse me?"

"Which English authors do you like best?"

For a moment she felt at a loss. She could tell him her favorite fruit, or her favorite color, but no one had ever asked her what writer she liked best.

"I'm not sure."

"Well, who have you read?"

"I've read many Agatha Christie books," she said tentatively, wondering if that would count since it wasn't on the list.

"I see," Carl Rosen said. They had just reached the second floor. As they approached the lab door, he spoke again. "And?"

"And other names?"

"Yes." He had a funny way of saying yes, Chie thought. He seemed to lean on it and draw it out. It sounded good when he said it. Inviting.

"Mark Twain. Sherlock Holmes." She'd once tried to read Jane Austen but found herself often unsure who was speaking. *The Catcher in the Rye* had been confusing.

"I see," he said, as he put the key into the door lock.

Once inside the lab, Chie immediately set about putting the materials on the tables and busied herself at the back of the room—as far as possible from the inquiring Carl Rosen.

"How nice of you to come," Kimiko said, in her phony-polite language. She could have as well said, "I invited you, and if you didn't show up, I would be through with you forever."

"I didn't have any problem finding it."

"Of course not. Stop acting like you're a little lost country girl," Kimiko said, much more in character. "You should know your way around the city."

Chie chose to pay no attention to this.

"Your place is really nice." She could see the whole apartment upon entering: the mini kitchen with mini dining area attached, and the one central room, with a white sofa.

"That opens out into a double bed," Kimiko said as she followed Chie's eyes around the room.

"Oh."

"Want something to drink?" Kimiko asked.

"Sure. Thanks."

"Well, what? Tea, juice, beer?"

"Tea is fine."

She watched Kimiko fill a red kettle with water and noticed that Kimiko had stayed with her colors. "You've decorated it very nicely," Chie said.

"I've decided red and white are my colors. It's bright."

"And it's so clean."

"It's new. And Mother comes once a week. She brings food and usually spends a couple of hours cleaning. And a good thing too. I'll do my laundry, but you're not going to find me cleaning a toilet." Kimiko poured tea. "Stay. We can have dinner together."

"Oh, I can't."

"Why not? You don't have a good reason."

Chie couldn't come up with what Kimiko would have called a good reason, and she didn't want to lie. If she had simply said the truth, that she wanted to go home to read, Kimiko would have laughed it off. When Kimiko offered to order out for soba—the buckwheat noodles were Chie's favorite—she agreed. And anyway, if she acquiesced this time, she could more easily beg off the next time Kimiko asked, and Chie knew there would be a next time. Kimiko, more bored than anything else, always seemed never to be able to stand her own company. While Chie usually felt there weren't enough hours in the day to read, to daydream, Kimiko, once she was through with a magazine, hardly knew why she was awake.

Chie called her mother to tell her not to save dinner and that she didn't need her father to pick her up at the station. She was already looking forward to her ride home on her bicycle in the cool darkness.

The delivery man rang the bell and handed Kimiko the tiered boxes of soba.

"Why three? Who's going to eat all this?" Chie asked, though she loved cool buckwheat noodles and thought she could manage it herself.

"Just in time," Kimiko said, answering the doorbell a second time. "Come on in," she said to a young man, short and thickset. "Kubota Takayuki, I'd like you to meet my oldest friend, Uchida Chie."

"Nice to meet you," they both said, bowing.

"So. Let's eat."

"I really must be going," Chie said, standing and gathering her things.

"Takayuki can see you to the station," Kimiko said. "He may be short, but he's strong. You can't see his muscles through his shirt, but they're big. That's from judo. He's *sho-dan*." Black belt.

Kimiko didn't see that she was embarrassing him, and she didn't seem to care that she embarrassed Chie.

"I'm fine. It's a short walk to the station," Chie said. "I'll see you at school." She turned to Takayuki and bowed.

He bowed in return, keeping his eyes lowered.

Chie was glad she hadn't had her father meet her at the station. She needed to think. Before she got to the house, and before she lay down for the night. After she passed the main street leading away from the station, the dark night enveloped her. The local government kept threatening to put in streetlamps, to bring the countryside in line with town policies. She could see the road well enough, and no one passed her. She was always glad the way to Uchida Road was one of the places where she could see the night sky without the interference of shop and streetlights.

It was clear Takayuki would be staying the night. Chie didn't even want to think about it. It wasn't her business or her concern. But should she talk to Kimiko about it? Among her friends, Kimiko was always the first to do something. The first to get her period. The first to wear lipstick. The first to say she'd kissed a boy. Perhaps Chie should do something, she kept thinking. Maybe she was partly responsible. After all, she had gone to that movie with her. It was like an endorsement.

"How was your day, dear?" her mother asked as soon as Chie walked in.

"Oh. Just fine. You really shouldn't have waited up," Chie said, knowing every evening her mother took her bath and was in her futon by eight o'clock.

"Oh, it's only eight thirty."

"But you get up at four."

"Never mind," her mother said, and reached for Chie's bag, as though she were reaching for the briefcase of a husband returning from the office. "And wasn't that nice of Kimiko to invite you?"

"Yes, it was nice. We had *zaru* soba."

"Oh, wasn't that sweet of her! Kimiko knows it's your favorite."

Sweet. Sweet? Is that the word her mother would use if she knew what Kimiko was doing? If she knew what she was really like?

"Um."

"Oh. Isao called. He'll be here for Golden Week."

"Oh great," Chie said, and meant it. It seemed he'd been gone so long, though really it was barely more than a month. But she always missed him when he wasn't around, even if he was away for a school trip of a few days. Isao was so solid, so simple. He never appeared confused or wracked by all the thoughts that kept her in a state of low-grade restlessness and indecision. And she wasn't even deciding anything. No choices had been offered yet. But she always had this overwhelming feeling that she had to make a decision. Make a move.

Still hot from the bath, Chie lay awake in her futon wondering what it would be like to love a man. She was a woman now and she knew it, she felt it. She desired what women desired. But how could she have it when she wasn't married and did not want to marry, not for a long time yet? She turned on her side, away from the open window, imagining she was turning into the arms of her love and being held in those arms. The arms were strong and warm, and she imagined stroking them. She was falling into sleep with a deep longing for the arms of Carl Rosen to embrace her in passion. And she was thoroughly ashamed. Oh, how could she feel this way about her sensei? Her teacher. A grown man. A man about whom she knew nothing. She cried in her confusion.

4

The following day in class Chie avoided looking at Carl Rosen, at all. She vowed to herself she would not her let their eyes meet, no matter what. Retreating quickly after the class was over, she was waylaid in the hall.

"Chie Uchida. And how are we today?"

Did he really say *we?*

"On your way to the library? Me too." She didn't have to look at him. As he came up alongside her in the hallway, she was already conscious of the dark olive color of his suit nearing her. "I'll walk with you."

Chie could hardly believe he had guessed her destination, informed her of his, and volunteered, unilaterally, to accompany her, all in one breath. She could not even guess at the correct reply or response to this behavior in English, or Japanese.

"I can't believe how hot it is already," he said. "I wonder if professors will be wearing suits throughout the summer." Turning to her, he asked, "Do you think it's necessary?"

Now her eyes met his. Hazel with a touch of gray, though she could swear they were a lighter shade yesterday, they matched his general coloring, and the suit. Realizing she was doing just what she said she wouldn't do, she looked down and away.

"I can't say. Perhaps you should do as the other professors do." No sooner were the words out of her mouth than she deeply regretted this exchange. He was asking her advice and she was supplying suggestions.

"Does it stay this hot all summer?"

It was impossible to avoid looking at him—in another second it would even be impolite. His way of communicating seemed to demand she look at him with her response. And not just at him, but into his eyes. They were a magnet and—against her will, it seemed—drew her in.

He held open the door to the library. Chie's thank-you was in a voice so small as to be inaudible.

"At least it's cool in here." He removed his jacket and draped it on the back of his chair. "We'll talk about the weather again sometime." He sat down, put his briefcase on the table, and took out a large book. "See you," he said, dismissing her.

"Goodbye," Chie said, and turned toward the bookshelves. She looked down at the cover of his book, and he noticed her glance. He closed the book, keeping his finger in the page he'd opened it to, and showed it to her.

"Cheever. His short stories. John Cheever, a very troubled man."

When Chie got home, Isao was already there. *Akarui*. Cheerful, bright. Sunny disposition, the word described him perfectly. And now after the stay at their aunt's farm in the north he seemed even more akarui.

"*Omae!*" he said, addressing her with the informal and impolite "you" as Chie put her head in the doorway of the central room. They often called each other omae. This rough word, used by men, was also used to indicate familiarity, closeness, and, especially, affection.

"Isao! You're back early!" Chie had hoped to get home before he came, to clean up a bit, to pick some flowers and display her small talents at ikebana she'd learned in the high school flower-arrangement club.

"I didn't want to arrive after dark. Besides, it's not so early. I just heard the five o'clock chime."

"Yeah, I guess it's not that early."

"I'd say it's late for you to be getting home from school. Do you have classes this late?"

"Most of my classes are in the morning. But I usually spend some time in the library reading." Chie immediately and involuntarily reminded herself of her meeting with Carl Rosen earlier. She hoped she wasn't blushing, but she could feel the color rising to her cheeks, and consciously turned away from Isao as she put her bag down.

"So, how're you? How's our aunt? How're the apples?"

Isao's good nature was demonstrated as he laughed out loud. No doubt he'd noticed her blush, but he would do anything rather than embarrass her, and he wouldn't dream of asking what might have caused her to blush. And although Chie was grateful, for a moment she wished he would ask. She wished she could talk to him, tell him what was on her mind. She wished she could say what she was feeling, what her body was feeling. It was all so new, and while this feeling was all-enveloping, she didn't have words for it. And even if she did, there was no one she would've talked to.

"Everybody up there is fine. It's incredibly cold, and it seems winter goes on forever. They're all used to it, of course, but it took me some time to adjust, and to learn to wear warm enough clothes! You won't believe it, but they're still sitting around the kotatsu!"

"In April?"

"April in Aomori is still winter. And I can count the days I saw the sun when I was there."

"Did you like the work?" Chie wasn't even sure why she asked this question. She knew it was farm work.

"Farm work is farm work. Whether it's apples, tea, or rice. It's farm work. But I did learn a lot, and they all seemed so impressed that I could carry such large loads. You know our uncle is only as big as Mother."

"Well, you are strong. I never thought my little brother would grow up to be this big." Chie gave his arm a squeeze. His muscular forearms, brown year-round from outdoor work, were defined beginning at the wrist and ending in a large bulge that formed the biceps. In that moment, Chie realized her little brother was a man. She let his arm go.

"But never mind all that stuff. How's school, college girl?"

"Oh, it's great. I love it."

"I can't believe Kimiko is in the same school. She's such a dolt." It wasn't like him to be unkind, but he did tend to say what he meant. "I know she's not in the English Department. What's she majoring in? Clothes?"

"She's in the business school, the Commerce Department."

"Kimiko? You must be joking!"

Not only was it highly unlikely Kimiko would ever work in an office, it was also impossible to imagine her having a job at all.

"She seems to like it."

"So, how do you like English? Can the teacher speak English?" Isao laughed. Chie laughed too, remembering that their junior high school English teacher struggled with English.

"The teacher is American. He's from New York."

"No kidding. What's he like?"

This was it. Chie felt warm all over now, not just her cheeks. She was suffocating. She began to feel she could not escape this Carl Rosen, even in her own home. But she was determined to.

"Let me get dinner started before Mother comes in. Come and help me."

"Me? The only son?" Isao followed her into the kitchen.

Their father, Hiroshi Uchida, was a man whose life followed a routine that was unchanging, except with the seasons. In the spring and summer, he had beer with his sashimi. In the fall and winter, this changed to warm sake. This regular evening indulgence while sitting alone at the low central table was what he most looked forward to after a day in the fields. In winter he kept warm wearing a thick quilted *hanten*, and in summer this changed to *jinbei*, the short, lightweight cotton pants and jacket. Out of nowhere, he'd begin talking: "I could not bear a stranger coming to live in my house," he'd state with conviction to no one but himself. "I can't tolerate a stranger living in my house." He'd declared this early, while Chie was still an adolescent—all in clear reference to the real possibility that she would marry, and her husband would be adopted into the family. And become head of the house.

Hiroshi Uchida could not even tolerate visitors. Occasions like the round of visiting relatives did at New Year's was notably unbearable to him. Relatives going from house to house, dropping in to make the customary holiday greetings, then staying to eat *o-sechi ryori,* the specialty food served in lacquer tiered boxes and on the finest ceramic ware dishes, used only once a year, was nothing he wanted to participate in. When most people were relaxing and welcoming their visitors, sitting around in a familiarity that combined the formal with the informal, Mr. Uchida would find something to do, at the back of the house, in the utility shed, just anywhere people were not.

The talk at dinner was all about Isao, about what he'd learned in that distant province. The parents were fascinated to hear about all the new farm equipment their relatives had, the pesticides and fungicides, labor-saving devices, and machines to do things they'd always done by hand.

Mrs. Uchida had taken out her fine set of sake cups in recognition this was a special meal since Isao was home, and after dinner Isao and his father poured each other warm sake in the miniature cups. Mr. Uchida preferred the cheap "One Cup" sake sold in glass jars—he kept every one of the jars, and the shed was full of them. He'd never answer the question of what he planned to do with them, but there was no thought he'd throw them out. There was something humorous about these two men—one small, wiry, tough with calloused hands, the other strapping, muscular, and with a touch of adolescent clumsiness—handling the elegant ceramic sake cups. Both of their faces had the unmistakable red glow of inebriation.

"Well, my son's a man now," their father pronounced as if a news bulletin to them all. "He's ready to take a wife."

Chie glared at her father. He must have really drunk too much, she thought. Whatever would make him think Isao was ready to be married? He was not yet twenty.

"Yes," their mother intoned from the kitchen, "he'll be starting his own family soon."

Chie could hardly believe her ears. Her mother, she knew, had not drank a drop. She'd never tasted alcohol in her life. But worst of all was Isao: he hadn't said even a peep in protest to this nonsense. No, the whole family wasn't drunk, but surely they'd gone mad.

5

C arl stepped out of the deep bath and rubbed himself hard with a thick towel that soaked up the water clinging to the heavy hair that carpeted his body. Wrapping himself in a *nemaki*, the gauze-cotton sleeping robe was like a blotter against his skin. He made a mental note: *buy more towels*. There was no clothes dryer, and in this humid climate, towels took days to dry, and even then, always felt damp. Now stretched out on his futon, he made another note to get a sofa, or at least a comfortable sitting chair. But in this moment, he was comfortable and relaxed—relaxed enough to think that, for the first time since he'd come to the city two months earlier, how alone he was. This wasn't the life he'd planned for himself. If he'd had a plan at all, it wasn't to be living alone in an unknown city in a foreign country. But he'd been in Japan before and knew that while it took some adjustment and getting used to, some obvious barriers could be penetrated—it was possible to make a life here.

After arriving in Takaizu, a city of half a million, he'd found an apartment he liked right away, half an hour's walk to the college. There was no shortage of housing choices, and he'd had his pick of at least five places. The agent who'd shown him apartments appeared confounded a single man was willing to pay the considerable difference in rent to live in a place that had more space than the agent thought he could use.

The view was mainly what Carl sought. The corner room of the third-floor apartment looked out over a lake that could be said to be the only attraction in this industrial city that had been leveled during the war. Though Takaizu could now boast a shiny new station, superexpress train stop, and a no-expense-spared renovation of its Edo-era castle, the city was otherwise nondescript and undistinguished. Carl had seen vintage photographs taken of the lake showing Seurat-like scenes of bathers and families picnicking on the banks. Now, badly polluted, the lake could only be enjoyed as something to look at from a distance. Takaizu, known for its many sunny days, promised a daily spectacular sunset from his window.

Telling the agent he'd take the three-bedroom apartment, and that the room overlooking the lake was perfect for a study, the thrifty agent had replied, "But my dear sir, why would you need a separate room to study when you have the whole place to study, as you are alone?" Carl could see no reason why he should offer an explanation, and only found it curious the agent would let sentimental solicitousness keep him from trying to make money on a rental deal.

The extra room would be for Carl's books. He had a lot of books. Carl was moderate in most things, owning no more clothes than what he wore, just enough underwear and socks to get him through until the next laundry. Books were different. He had to have the books he wanted to read, had heard about, read about, read reviews of, might like to read, had long meant to read—books that possibly contained information he might need, or perhaps a quote he hoped not to forget. And his library was made up of many books he had already read, lent, lost, and replaced. It was important to him to possess books, and the boxes of books that had been delivered when he moved in were still stacked on the floor of the room that would be his study. Going shopping in search of bookcases, he was sorry the choice was so limited. The six cases he ended up buying, chest-high with just three shelves, stood empty. He was waiting for the day he'd have enough time to put the books on the shelves, in order —a methodical order of novels, short stories, plays, biography, autobiography, poetry. When he reached for a book, he wanted it to be right where he expected. At the same time, he often enjoyed finding a book he wasn't looking for as he searched for another book.

There was never a time he was not in the middle of a book. Still, though he was someone who read constantly, no one would have described Carl Rosen as bookish.

Now, stretched out on the futon, a hand and elbow supporting his head, he read *The Inland Sea*. He was not familiar with the author, Donald Richie, but thought this writer, who had adopted Japan as his home, might be a good guide. His book was intriguing, as it appeared the writer was discovering and uncovering the country at the same time. Soon distracted by the discomfort of his reading position, Carl vowed on the spot to furnish the apartment properly. He was not going to be camping out here, he told himself. He had no need to affix the word *home* to this place or even this country, but for however long it was going to be, he wanted it to be comfortable.

Years earlier he would have hardly given it a thought. The way he lived and how and where he slept made little difference to him back then. In Malaga, in Spain, he'd slept on a lumpy straw mattress for more than a year. After he moved to a small town bordering the Pyrenees in France, for six months his bed had been a sleeping bag on a tile floor. But then, he rarely slept alone. Before arriving in Takaizu, he'd made up his mind he was going to have a life in this new place. No lonely teacher in one room, eating warmed-over food in a not-quite-fresh shirt. He was familiar with the makeshift life, and he'd had enough of it.

Carl closed his book and sat up. It was still early enough to call Sakai-san.

"Your wife seemed really surprised I speak Japanese," Carl said when Toshinaga Sakai came to the phone. "She seemed astonished. What did you tell her about me?"

"Not much. Just that you were the new English teacher."

"But she knows I didn't just get 'off the boat,' right?"

"Well," and Sakai-san laughed, "I didn't tell her anything. I just said the new teacher might be joining us. So. Are you coming?"

"That's why I called." And then, slipping into formal Japanese like a glove, "If it wouldn't be too much of an imposition, I'd be honored to join you and your family."

"Terrific," Sakai said, his choice of words and Midwestern accent still intact from his high school days as an overseas exchange student in Indiana. And then in Japanese, "You're so formal. You're impossible when you speak Japanese."

"You are my *sempai*," Carl said, acknowledging the status difference since Sakai-san had been at the college longer.

"We're not going to pay attention to any of that stuff. Okay. So, tomorrow, we'll pick you up."

"No, no," Carl protested. "I'll walk over to your house. I know where it is."

"Walk? It'll take you an hour."

"No, it won't. It's not that far. What time should I be there?"

"Is ten too early?"

"See you at ten a.m."

Sipping a beer as he came to the end of *The Inland Sea*, he thought he might give it a reread. But for now, he felt the warmth and promised satisfaction of knowing he'd be getting together with his friend Sakai and his family. Yes, he thought to himself, he was going to have a life now. Maybe he, too, would adopt this country as his home.

"Please come in."

My god, she's beautiful.

"Carl. Good of you to come." Sakai appeared from a side room and put out his arm in the gesture of an offering. "This is my wife, Yoshiko."

Carl and Yoshiko bowed to each other, exchanging conventional greetings.

"And my children. Son, Yoshinaga. Daughter, Yui."

"Hello. Nice to meet you," they said in unison.

"And nice to meet you," Carl said, putting out a hand to match little outstretched hands. "And how nice you speak English."

"That's it from them. Until I teach them to memorize something else. Come on in, come in." Toshinaga led Carl into a room to the right of the entrance hall.

The room had the fresh-straw smell of new tatami. The

wood trim gleamed, the few items in it were purposefully and beautifully placed.

"It's still new," Sakai said. "We haven't been in this house even a year yet. Just about eight months. And of course, we never use this room."

Carl looked at the calligraphy scroll hanging in the *tokonoma*, the alcove that also held a flower arrangement of fresh azaleas.

"Yoshiko does all this stuff," Toshinaga volunteered. "She's a true *ojousama*. A carefully brought-up daughter of a well-to-do family, where daughters are raised to be professionals. Professional wives, that is."

Yoshiko appeared at the door on silent feet, soundlessly going to her knees as she put a tray with teapot and cups beside her on the tatami. She poured Carl's tea, handing it to him with two hands. Her fingers, tapered like a doll's, barely seemed to touch the translucent porcelain cup.

Although she was not a conventionally pretty woman, Yoshiko's features could be described as exquisite, like a Noh mask. Wide-set eyes, appearing as if they'd been painted on by a master doll-maker, sat above a nose sculpted for her perfectly symmetrical face. Lips designed for her small mouth, free of lipstick, were yet full of color.

She withdrew her slender body as silently as she had brought it in, and Toshinaga called out, "Come and sit down with us. This is a harmless *gaijin*!" The children giggled, and the lightness of the moment signaled they didn't have to sit in the formal *seiza* position on the silk cushions any longer. Simultaneously stretching their legs, they reached for the rice crackers that had been served.

"How lucky you are." Carl took a sip of his tea. "Son and daughter, new house. Beautiful wife."

"I have a huge loan. You can be this 'lucky' too!"

"Speak in English, Papa," his son said. "We want to hear you speak in English to Rosen-san."

"I'll make a fool of myself. His Japanese is perfect."

"Then why did we have to speak in English?"

"So you could practice. I don't know when you'll get another chance to greet someone in English."

Yoshiko came back in, as instructed. Carl noticed she'd removed her apron.

"It is really nice of you to join us," she said.

"It was nice of Toshi to invite me."

"That's more like it. Call me Toshi." He turned to his wife. "That's what all the fellows called me when we were at the seminar. We only used first names. It was great."

"Have you been in Japan long?" Yoshiko asked.

"Oh. A while," Carl answered, purposely vague. "Mostly in the north. In Nagano. It's beautiful there. But so cold."

"As it happens, Yoshiko is from Nagano. And she can't take cold weather at all. Nothing colder than spring."

"Then Takaizu's temperate climate must be perfect for you," Carl said.

"Yes, I prefer it to the north."

"I admire your calligraphy," Carl said. "You're obviously an expert. Do you also write *kana*?" He knew she would. Those slender fingers would surely write the finest of Japanese calligraphy. Kana. the delicate writing at which women excelled.

"Oh, do you do calligraphy?" Yoshiko looked at him directly for the first time.

"I've tried. But just *kaisho*, like all children learn. These thick fingers couldn't hold the fine brush needed for kana. They're more suited to hold a hammer, and I'm no good at that either."

"Oh, but that's quite wonderful you've practiced calligraphy." A small smile appeared on her perfect lips.

"That'll do with the Japanese cultural appreciation class. Let's get down to the beach," Toshi broke in.

"Yes. The sooner we get there, the sooner we'll be able to leave. Before the crowds," Yoshiko said as she gathered up the tea things.

Carl was surprised when Yoshiko didn't sit in the driver's seat. She seemed to be the one in charge. She'd left the house reminding her husband to change his shirt and to take the camera and telling him where the children should be dropped off for their different playdates.

Toshi told Carl the kite festival was his favorite of Japan's many festivals. He'd said his father had enthusiastically spent an enormous sum to sponsor a kite in Toshi's name when he was born, and that he and his father went to the festival every year throughout his boyhood.

"My mother never came. She couldn't stand the crowds. She thought of it as a gathering of brutes."

At first Carl thought he wouldn't be able to take the crowds either. Thousands of people trampled on the beach, their feet beating the sand as the strong wind for which the area was known sent the sand dust swirling in their faces. Rough men in black leggings, black canvas split-toe work shoes, and *happi* coats emblazoned with the insignia of their neighborhoods sent kites soaring, battling other kites sent aloft in mock battle. The kites, each one a work of art, were striking. With their great size, impressive with bold character lettering in sharp contrast with vivid background colors and designs, they stood out against an overcast sky and wide gray ocean backdrop.

"They get too crazy these days," Toshi said. "There really is a lot of skill involved in flying a kite well, but these days guys have lost it. Most of them never had it."

The goal was to fly the kite very high very fast so that its taut line of handspun hemp would saw through any kite it contacted.

"Now they try to bring the kites down in a tangle of lines." And when they did, Toshi explained, all that was left of these stunning handcrafted kites were scraps of rice paper and bits of bamboo.

Carl thoroughly enjoyed the spectacle, but he also thought it a great pity to destroy those magnificent kites. He wondered that men would make something so beautiful, so splendid—delicate, really—just to destroy it.

Yoshiko appeared to be taking it all in good-humoredly, trudging along with them in the sand. She seemed too fragile to be anywhere near where men were having their battles, mock or not. Carl noticed a fine layer of sand dust on her dark hair, which was pulled back from her face, revealing a semicircular hairline. He wanted to get her out of there.

"Are you enjoying it?" he asked.

"Oh yes. I like excitement."

. . .

Yoshiko Kawakami had grown up as the only daughter of a sake merchant. The Kawakami family's store, which they could boast had remained in the same location for two hundred years, was a source of pride for the family, and the whole community. During the war, their town, known for its charming traditional beauty, had been spared from the bombs. Her father had taken this as a sign—of what he wasn't sure, but he believed it signaled he was meant to prosper. And so it seemed. While Japan was still at war and the entire country subsisted on a diet of *satsumaimo*, the Kawakami family field yielded more of these sweet potatoes than the average. Despairing, one shopkeeper wanted to trade the entire stock of dried fish and seaweed he'd stored for a few barrels of sake.

Yoshiko had indeed been raised as a true ojousama, precious daughter. Her parents saved the best morsels of food for her, and she somehow seemed to miraculously escape any of the childhood diseases that plagued so many malnourished children in the early years after the war. She'd had a brother who succumbed to tuberculosis before the war's end. Long before her parents could truly afford it, she was given the best of everything. For her mother, the highest station the Kawakami family could attain was for her daughter to marry well, preferably a doctor, or a man who was successful in his own business. As for her father, his only wish was that his only daughter marry as a virgin. Neither of these wishes was to be granted.

Yoshiko had all the aesthetic lessons that denoted good breeding, and her certificates, awarded after each achievement, piled up. By the time she left high school, she was already qualified to be a wife, as far as her mother was concerned. She didn't just have cooking lessons, but lessons in preparing *kaiseki*, the highly specialized Japanese cuisine that is as much an art form as it is food. In addition to the lessons in calligraphy, wearing kimono, and flower arrangement, naturally she was taught tea ceremony, which encompassed all the other lessons. Allowing her to go to junior college would be just an extra—unnecessary, as far as her parents could see. But they recognized it would make her that much more prized. Her mother was beside herself with rage when Yoshiko insisted on going to a four-year college. It had been her plan from the beginning, and keeping to her resolve, her parents had no choice but to relent. For Yoshiko, marriage was a possibility but never part of a plan. When she met Toshinaga Sakai he was in the last year of college. She had two more years and thought that, if she were going to marry, he might indeed be perfect. She liked that, though he was an academic who might one day be considered an expert in his field, Japanese literature, he had none of the put-on airs of the professors she'd known. Most especially, not only did he worship her, but he also accepted her just as she was. She thought of him as the man who would not try to change anything about her, which said a lot because, despite the traditional way she was raised, she was in no way traditional.

They entered the *sushiya*, but instead of sitting at the sushi shop's counter as they usually did, Yoshiko led them to the one small table set off in the corner. Toshi ordered sake as soon as they sat down, and she poured for Carl and Toshi when the server set it on the table.

"You like sake?" Carl politely took the small decanter from her hands and poured for her in turn.

"Yes, quite a bit," she said, and sipped from the small *chokko*. "This sake is too sweet for my taste. For Toshi it's all the same. When he ordered he didn't ask for a specific brand. That might be why they served us *amakuchi*, a sweet one."

"This is our favorite place. If we eat sushi, we only eat here," Toshi said. He picked up a piece of pale red tuna that had just been set before him, turned it upside down to dip in the soy sauce, and plopped it into his mouth in one piece.

"It's good sushi," Carl said, his thick fingers repeating the same action. "And the rice is not too vinegary."

"Do you know about Japanese cuisine?" Yoshiko asked, recalling his comments about the different kinds of *tare*, sauces for yakitori, the skewered grilled chicken they ate from *yatai*, portable food stands, at the festival earlier. "Do you cook?"

"No. But I used to. Actually, I studied Japanese cooking, once upon a time."

"Is that so?"

"But I never learned to make sushi."

Yoshiko poured them another round of sake and then ordered more, this time asking for the one she wanted by name.

"You know your sake, I see," Carl said.

"She ought to. She's the daughter of sake merchants. Generations of them."

"Really? Where in Nagano are you from?"

"Matsumoto. The Japan Alps. It's famous for *daiginjo*, which is really the best sake to drink with sushi." As soon as she said this, she realized there was no need to elucidate geographical and culinary facts. It was becoming increasingly clear this gaijin knew Japan, and things Japanese, well.

The city of Matsumoto had been Carl's first experience of Japan. As a young exchange student he'd stayed with the Arai family at their home in the city's center. Their house was so small that from the minute he entered, he wondered that they would open it to a stranger. But they did, unreservedly. Mrs. Arai prepared wonderful meals and *obento*, lunch boxes, she insisted were "common," but it was all new and special to Carl. In addition to the daily culinary delights, he was introduced to their neighbors and relatives and regularly taken on day trips to other parts of Nagano prefecture. Treating him like a son from the beginning, the family spoke to him only in Japanese, ensuring Carl would be a competent, if not yet fluent, speaker, by the time the homestay ended.

Carl watched as Yoshiko sipped her sake, taking small bites of the sushi. He didn't know how old Yoshiko was, but he was sure she was younger than him. Looking at her now, he imagined she'd been one of the giggling schoolgirls who'd pointed and stared at him when he well might have been the only foreigner in Matsumoto, sticking out like a big American thumb. At first he'd been annoyed, but then amused, when his homestay sister told him the girls undoubtedly just thought he was *kawaii*, cute.

Yoshiko was curious about this American teacher. Long before she met him, she'd heard about him from Toshi, who talked about Carl not just in admiring terms, but as though he were some special breed of man. Toshi could hardly stop talking about him, saying Carl was the "*genki* guy," the most spirited member of a seminar Toshi led the summer before. According to him, Carl "knew everything," never saying specifically what it was he knew. And Toshi bestowed on him the greatest accolade that he could: "His Japanese is better than mine."

"It's curious you were in Toshi's Japanese course," Yoshiko said, though that was not at all what she was curious about. "You don't need to study Japanese at all."

"Toshi's course was particularly valuable for me because we weren't just studying Japanese language, but literature. And at that time, I was planning on returning to the States to teach Japanese."

"Oh?"

"But when Toshi got in touch and told me he'd gotten the college to add an English literature seminar to the curriculum, and the teaching position was mine if I wanted it, I thought it was an opportunity too good to pass up."

The rest of the evening was spent talking about everything but what Yoshiko wanted to talk about. Not one word was uttered about what she was interested to know: Was he married? Had he been married? Were there children? Who was his wife? Was she Japanese? American? What had happened? She knew it was impossible to initiate conversation on any subject like this and participated in the talk with a restraint that wasn't difficult to assume. Still, she was curious. But common Japanese social conventions, as well as Carl's averted eyes, guaranteed his personal circumstances would not be under discussion.

The doors of the sushiya were open, and they could hear the drumming and tinny tooting of badly played cheap trumpets as festival revelers made their way through downtown Takaizu. Though the sound was still distant, the noise was a sign the revelers were working themselves into a frenzy of energy that propelled them along in the night. When the night came to an end, they'd drape their arms around each other's shoulders, spinning in a circle, a primitive whirling of bodies holding up bodies.

By the time they left, Yoshiko had spent a good part of the evening looking at Carl's hands, not at all sure why they attracted her attention, attracted her. Obviously, she noticed he wasn't wearing a wedding band, but that didn't mean anything: she and Toshi had never worn wedding rings. Carl walked with them back to the car. Opening the car door, he touched Yoshiko's arm just above the elbow, before continuing on his way to his apartment. Now, lying in bed after a soak in the bath, she wondered that she could still feel the impression of his fingers on her skin.

In Yoshiko's world, the world of a married woman with children, a Japanese housewife, it was unthinkable that she would associate with men her age. The husbands of the women she knew and could call friends were strangers to her. Indeed, she doubted she'd recognize any of them should she pass them on the street. The man who delivered the rice, the postman who most often brought their mail, the son of the owner of the vegetable market were probably the only men close to her in age with whom she regularly came into contact. The barriers that existed between men and women were simple and invisible, but they were there and could be seen every time men and women self-segregated in the most innocuous situations. The few times she'd met the husbands of her friends, the odd times when those men were at home or when they attended some school sports event, she'd been tempted to flirt just for the fun of it. In all probability she'd never lay eyes on them again. Sometimes she'd smile to herself that she even entertained the possibility of starting an affair. Yoshiko had thought about this many times. And it was not that she wanted to have an affair, it was more just the excitement of something out of reach.

Now, with the American Carl Rosen, although she'd only just met him, already she felt he could be a friend, and she liked the idea of having a man as a friend. Toshi had been that. But it was clear from the beginning that he wanted marriage. With Carl it would be something to explore, and in her head she devised situations where they could get together, like having him participate in their family gatherings. She believed she'd be able to uncover mutual interests, and thereby he could become a personal friend. And all this because he was a foreigner. It was almost like he didn't count.

6

Customarily during the five-day holiday known as "Golden Week" the Uchidas took a trip. They'd visit relatives who lived nearby, or not far. The ones who lived furthest would not see the Uchidas' faces until there was a marriage or funeral, events for which all the women had appropriate kimono at the ready. Sometimes, to please Mrs. Uchida, the family would spend a night at an inn with *onsen*, natural hot springs. When they did, Mr. Uchida complained about it all: Who knows who slept on the futon before them? The food, no matter how splendid, also had him concerned: Who could say who'd prepared it? The irascible Mr. Uchida often seemed on the verge of sending his wife, these rare occasions when she got to be served, into the inn's kitchen.

This year during Golden Week they stayed at home, mostly sitting around the small central table, and this year most of the talk centered on Isao. He would not be going back to his aunt's place in Aomori. Instead, his father had arranged an apprenticeship for him at the local lumber mill of still another relative. As a result of a government forest-expansion campaign, all the beech trees native to their area had been decimated and replanted with conifers that were more economical for building. It was thought that Isao's learning about this burgeoning industry would be a kind of insurance in the event the Uchida's farm didn't prosper. The important thing was that Isao be able to provide for a wife and family, and comfortable enough to look after his parents as they aged.

Although the first talk of her little brother taking a wife had been too much for her to even think about, now Chie had adjusted to it and even thought it was a good idea. With the dependable Isao settled, she wouldn't need to be concerned about her parents. While it was not possible Chie could completely disregard the responsibility of her position as the eldest, from early years it had been obvious to her and accepted by Isao that he, though the younger, would assume the responsibility of their parents as they grew old. Now, Chie could sense the possibility of leaving this small world of the *inaka*, the Japanese countryside, with all its built-in limits and predetermined fates. She could feel her life on Uchida Road start to recede, and it made her think her dreams might no longer just be daydreams.

On the second day of the holiday, Chie sat with her father and Isao while they drank after-dinner sake.

"Of course there are available women nearby, right here on Uchida Road, in fact," Mr. Uchida said, though there had not been talk about "available women" near or far. "But my brother has two women he wants to introduce."

Neither Chie nor Isao responded. And they didn't need to ask which of their father's five brothers he was talking about, because it was the eldest, who was a teacher, that their father held in the highest esteem.

"My elder brother tells me they are both women born in the Year of the Dog." As these women are supposed to be distinguished for their patience, reliability, and selflessness, it was considered not just a good year for a woman to be born, but the best. "They will make good wives. You can count on it."

"Father, I would not consider an arranged marriage," Isao said, not hiding his strong aversion to the idea.

"Not consider? I never heard such nonsense," Mr. Uchida said.

"I've met a woman, in Aomori," Isao announced. "Tomomi Hongo. She's the daughter of our aunt's friend."

Isao described meeting Tomomi when he went with his aunt and her good friend to make an offering at the local shrine during the spring festival. "Do you know what the first thing she said to me when we were introduced? 'Oh Isao, you're too formal! Don't call me Hongo-*san* or Tomomi-*san*. Our families are old friends!'"

"Well, she's certainly friendly!" Chie said. "She sounds like a lovely young woman."

"Chie, Tomomi and I got along so well together. It was like we'd known each other forever. I know you'll all like her." Isao had always been easygoing, and while possessing a strong character, he did not express strong opinions. But now he spoke in a sure voice, as if he were making a vow not to be broken. Turning to his father Isao said: "Tomomi is the woman I plan to marry."

"How can you stand there and tell your father who you plan to marry?" Their father's face, already red from the sake, got redder still with anger. Clearly drunk, he was also clearly enraged and startled them all with the loudness of his voice. "Is this the son I've raised?"

"Father, I'm not standing. We're all sitting together," Isao said, trying to make light of the moment. "And I am sure you will be happy with the woman I chose."

"How insolent you are!" Mr. Uchida yelled, accidentally knocking over the *tokkuri*, the ceramic sake decanter.

Chie set it right. Her mother, who had escaped to the kitchen at the first sign of unpleasantness, was now at Chie's side. She handed Chie a cloth to wipe up the spill, and then quickly retreated with the wet cloth to the safe harbor of the kitchen once again.

"Father," Chie said in a soothing voice one might use with a child, her language respectful, "I am sure you, as we all, desire Isao's happiness above all else."

"I should say not! Above all else? You sound like a madwoman! What about the fields? The rice and tea? The mikan? I suppose I should just let them take care of themselves while my son is busy being happy!"

Both Chie and Isao laughed, and Chie was certain she could hear her mother's small smiling murmur from the kitchen.

"Father. I will look after them as I have always intended. I will not disappoint you." Isao reached for the decanter to pour his father another cup of sake. Hesitating as he picked it up, he then moved it to the edge of the table, out of his father's line of vision.

"Well," his father started. "Well, this is all well and good. But what, I ask you . . . what am I to tell my eldest brother?"

Chie felt a tinge of sadness hearing her father express his bafflement, knowing he was truly bewildered. But she was firm in her reply: "That your son has found a woman he loves and will marry her."

The days following this talk were centered around how the young woman, Tomomi Hongo, would be properly introduced to the family. This presented more than a few conundrums: Should she come to their house? Should they go to hers? If she should come, should she be accompanied by just her mother or both parents? Since she had two younger sisters at home, should the Uchidas expect them to come too, or should they specifically invite them to come along? As the Hongo family would be coming far, perhaps the Uchida family should help defray the expenses. They could not possibly expect these guests to stay in the Uchida's old farmhouse, which prompted them to think they should book rooms in town, near the station for convenience. Or choose another hotel, though not as conveniently located, but newer. Since Isao had already met Tomomi's parents, maybe the right thing to do would be for the Uchidas themselves to go to Aomori, which was quite far. But, as the Uchidas were the elder couple, Tomomi's parents could not dream of asking them to do that without insulting them, which meant the Hongos would have to insist on going to the Uchidas, but then, that might be perceived as too forward.

Chie participated in this talk to the extent she could but could not help but feel removed from these mundane and, she thought, outdated concerns that bordered on the ridiculous. She knew there was no way of getting it across to her parents that it wasn't really necessary any longer, not in 1969, to be concerned with all these formalities and politenesses, protocols and "shoulds." They clearly had no awareness that these days quite a few women knew their future husbands before marrying, even intimately, even with no intention of marrying. She could have even given the example of Kimiko, who was so "sweet" according to her mother, though Chie never would have said a word about her.

She knew they would work it out. Perhaps other parties might be called in to negotiate, or both sets of parents would go over everything, no matter how many telephone calls or letters it took, until it was all resolved to everyone's satisfaction. It had already been agreed that their father could save face with his elder brother by letting the brother be *nakodo*, go-between, for Isao and Tomomi. Long before he laid eyes on Tomomi, as go-between he would be credited with arranging the introduction and marriage of his younger brother's son.

All the talk and machinations gave her family a busyness and excitement that was unusual in their normal lives. Chie wanted to be helpful but knew her input was not necessary. No one noticed the times she slipped away from the table and out of the room to go for walks behind the house on the weed-covered paths that led nowhere.

Chie was glad when classes started again after the holiday, glad to get back to what she loved. The last assignment Carl Rosen had given the class was a composition. "I know how difficult it will be to do it in English," he'd told them. Chie wondered if he knew how difficult it would have been to do in Japanese. Neither she nor the other students had any experience at all writing what Professor Rosen had repeated several times: "Your thoughts. Your feelings. Your impressions."

"It'll be a challenge," he'd said, as though that were a good thing. "Don't be afraid. I will not grade you harshly. I am not as concerned with your grammar and spelling as I am with your thoughts."

He told the class he'd be available to help them on an individual basis, and they should check the posted schedule of his office hours, tacked to the door of his office.

"All you need to do is write in your name and come to my office at the appointed time. With your work, of course." Looking directly at Chie he added, "I'm sure you all know my office is in the library building."

Chie hadn't been the least bit afraid to write the paper. If anything, she thought it would be a relief for her because she had been thinking so much about the books she was reading. But she couldn't help but think it a little scary when Professor Rosen said, "Writing is a way of sharing."

"Good afternoon, Chie Uchida" is how Carl Rosen greeted her when she went to his office the day following the end of the holiday. "Your name was the first name down."

He'd barely glanced at the door when she knocked and walked in. Instead he continued whatever he was writing. Now, putting his pencil down, he looked up at her, catching her eyes by surprise. "So, you really like reading and writing."

Chie, not sure if she'd been asked a question, not sure if she should give an answer, just stood there with Carl Rosen looking at her.

"Have a seat. Let me see what you have."

"How do you do?" she said, sitting down, and realizing she hadn't uttered a word since entering the room.

"I'm doing just fine. And you?"

"Oh," she said, "I'm sorry. I mean, good afternoon."

They both laughed, and his laugh mingling with hers made her relax.

"Your English is really quite good. You needn't be nervous. Or shy or afraid."

"Oh, thank you," she said, and immediately thought that might not be the right response.

"So. Let me see what you have." Carl held out his hand for the folder she carried. He glanced at the title and thumbed through the pages, turning to the last.

"I see you've written quite a bit. Three pages is a lot." He flipped back to the first page and skimmed it. "Let's meet again after I take it home and read it. But first, tell me why you chose *Under The Net*."

"I understood that students could choose freely from the reading list any book they wanted to write their composition on."

"Yes. Of course. I just want to know why you chose this particular book. What was your reason? Did you think it would be interesting, entertaining, exciting?"

Chie was silent. She did not expect this question and did not have an answer prepared. For their next meeting, she wanted to be able to reply.

Later in the week, she waited outside his office, as she could hear two people talking in Japanese, and she realized he had visitors.

When Carl Rosen came to the door, she stood aside waiting for a second person to leave.

"Come in, come in," Carl said. Chie hesitated and he looked at her. "Yes?"

"I thought there were two people here."

"There were."

"But only one left the room. Where is the other person?"

"Right here."

On the train ride home, Chie's confused feelings moved between humiliation and betrayal. Why didn't he tell her he could speak Japanese? She'd assumed he couldn't. He'd announced on the first day he would only speak English with the students in his class, and he didn't tell them he could speak Japanese. But now knowing he was fluent in Japanese, it was almost as if he could also read her mind.

She'd been feeling sorry for him, thinking he was a man alone in a new and foreign country, unable to speak the language, needing to adjust to unfamiliar surroundings, probably lonely. But he didn't sound lonely. The person he'd been talking to in his office was Sakai-sensei, and she had overheard them making plans to go to a concert. And then she thought it would have been so much easier for her if they'd discussed her composition in Japanese, instead of having her struggle to make herself clear in English. The worst thing was that she knew when she spoke English she had to say more, to expose more. She couldn't use any of her language's many escape hatches.

_____

7

Y oshiko couldn't remember the last time she had gone out in the evening. Like all her mother friends, her life was centered around the home and children. A social occasion might be a two-hour lunch with another mother—they never went out at night. The advent of Carl Rosen might change her world.

Yoshiko loved jazz. During the years she'd lived in Tokyo while attending college, going to small jazz clubs was her main social activity. She had no interest and didn't participate in the many university societies and associations, the weekend hiking and biking. She couldn't remember the many times she'd been asked to join this group or that club. Mostly she went to hear local bands at clubs where "intimate" better described the size rather than the atmosphere. It was something of a miracle the clubs managed to survive and the musicians managed to stay together long enough until they could sound like a group. She'd met a few of these musicians and knew some earned their living during daylight hours at securities firms and insurance companies or as department store managers. One trombonist she dated for a short time was a trader on the Tokyo Stock Exchange. Jazz piano was what she came to like the most, and although she could play a few standards, she disliked mediocre tinkling, including her own. She preferred those pianists who played what they could play, rather than make overly earnest, ostentatious efforts to imitate Bud Powell, Bill Evans, McCoy Tyner. Just two days after Carl's visit, she was excited to read in the paper that the Kenny Drew Trio was making a rare tour, and she quickly looked to see what cities in Japan they'd be visiting. She could hardly believe it when she saw Takaizu, not a regular stop for touring musicians, among them. Yoshiko called right away to reserve three seats.

"Oh no, not a jazz concert!" had been Toshi's response when she told him.

"Doesn't he like jazz?"

"Who?"

Yoshiko had forgotten she hadn't mentioned that she planned to invite Carl. She'd bought the tickets before asking, thinking that at the worst she'd lose a thousand yen, which seemed like a small loss compared to the possibility that she might not be able to get a ticket for him if she delayed.

"Oh, I thought Professor Rosen would like to join us. I thought I'd mentioned that I planned to include him."

"Please don't refer to him as Professor Rosen. He's my friend. Our friend. Call him Carl."

"Of course. I will. It's only that I am just getting know him. Toshi, please telephone and invite him."

Toshi telephoned and reported to Yoshiko that Carl was very happy to accept, and had said he didn't know Toshi liked jazz.

"I had to tell him that I don't, and this is your idea."

.   .   .

It was in Yoshiko's character to be thoughtful and considerate. Growing up at a time when people regularly inquired after their nearest neighbors, she had also regularly accompanied her mother to neighbors' houses to bring a meal to someone who had been ill. When their elderly next-door neighbor's husband died, Yoshiko's mother brought a hot meal every evening to the widow's house. Yoshiko ran errands for her and fed her cat until the woman herself died, one year after her husband.

Yoshiko knew Carl was alone, and she imagined he was lonely. And she knew that while he might know any number of people in Japan, she and Toshi were the only people he knew in Takaizu. That's the part she told her husband. She didn't tell him, she couldn't, that there had hardly been a day since she'd met Carl Rosen that she hadn't thought about him. And while there were opportunities for her to invite him to their home, she had the desire to establish a relationship among the three of them, as one outside the house, away from the family concerns that filled her life. Sure, there would be occasions when they'd meet at home, include the children, but she wanted this relationship to start out different.

They'd arranged to meet in front of the concert hall. While Toshi and Yoshiko waited, they saw several people they knew. Considering the population of Takaizu was close to half a million, it was like a small town, Yoshiko thought, as she nodded at yet another passing familiar face. With his dark hair and complexion and average height, Carl didn't stand out, but maybe it was because of his walk—he seemed to move sideways —she could spot him coming a block away.

He greeted them both with a bow, and then in a complete turnaround, like the agility he was capable of with language, he looked at Yoshiko full in the face and said enthusiastically, "I love jazz! How did you know?"

"I didn't. I hoped you would. I mean, I thought you might."

"Toshi, I guess you never told her about me and my jazz collection." He turned to Yoshiko as he explained. "I always listen to jazz. The program director's room was opposite mine, and he said that my constant playing of jazz was his only complaint in the six weeks we were all together. I don't play it loud, but I do play it all the time."

Carl was thoroughly animated now. He seemed much more upbeat than how Yoshiko had first perceived him. He didn't appear to be quite the pensive professor, the solitary character, she'd initially met.

"By the way," Carl said as they found their seats, "I've heard Kenny Drew play many times, in Copenhagen. That's where he lives."

"Really?" was all Yoshiko could think to say. But she wanted to know more. So much more. She'd heard him mention Spain, but there had been no talk of Copenhagen, of Denmark.

Taking their seats, Toshi told them about the hall, how it had been built when he was still a young boy, and how it had been the most modern and showiest building around.

"Yeah, I can see that," Carl said, eyebrows raised at the outdated design.

"The acoustics are still good, but these seats are small and cramped. I remember when I was a kid coming here, everything was so spacious and shiny. It was like a fantasy."

Seated between Toshi and Carl, before the concert was over, Yoshiko had to move her thighs a dozen times, clamping her legs together, to keep them from brushing against Carl's.

. . .

In early summer, a man walked on the moon.

Carl didn't have a television and didn't particularly care about this first-time feat, but Toshi called, saying Yoshinaga and Yui, beside themselves with excitement, wanted him to view it with them: "He's American!" The children's enthusiasm could be felt when he arrived at the Sakai's door and they yelled "Yay! He's here!" as though he were one of the astronauts. For his part, Carl was just happy to participate in another of their family's get-togethers. After ordering out for sushi, Yoshiko, Toshi, and Carl celebrated the momentous occasion with more than a few toasts of sake and beer.

By the time the college started the second of its three terms at the beginning of September, Carl had settled into a life he'd hardly imagined would have been possible for him. He had never been content to be alone before, but now he was living alone, liking it, and totally satisfied with his home arrangement. His daily routine included an early morning walk at the lake. At the height of summer, it was necessary to be out at the crack of dawn to try to avoid the heat, and now this quiet time in the early morning was the best part of his day.

He made friends with, or rather, had charmed any number of local shop ladies. These grandmothers loved the attention, and both he and they enjoyed the daily exchanges about the weather and the prices of food. And although he thought the food, especially vegetables and fruit, were expensive, he loved to exaggerate the price and then go on at length about how much cheaper it was in the States.

"And in California, you wouldn't believe it, they sell peaches by the bucket. They can't sell them cheap enough.

You've got to make pies, jam, cobbler." He found himself trying to describe peach cobbler as the shop women, and their husbands, too, looked at him with wide-eyed amazement.

One day the owner of the vegetable store at the end of his street took him aside and, practically whispering, said, "Rosen-san, what is this?"

Carl hadn't known what he might expect when the man held up a zucchini.

"I'm embarrassed to tell my customers I don't know what it is. And of course, I can't imagine how it should be cooked. What can I tell my customers?"

"That they're delicious and great as tempura."

"Please, Rosen-san. Just take them away. You can have the whole box."

Carl protested, but the greengrocer insisted.

That same day, Carl went to Toshi's office to invite the whole family over for ratatouille. Toshi couldn't repeat the name to Yoshiko but told her Carl had said there would be plenty, and to bring the children too.

Carl was a good cook, and he'd made up his mind when he moved to Takaizu that he wouldn't be eating some miserable bachelor diet. He detested instant and fast food and had no intention of cooking up a large pot of something on a Sunday, and then eating from it the rest of the week.

When the Sakai family showed up at dinnertime the following day, they were astonished to see the table he'd set.

"I see you like *Mashiko-yaki*," Yoshiko said, naming the ceramic ware that was also one of her favorites.

"I prefer *Arita-yaki*, but I'm pretty clumsy with these thick fingers. I like that Mashiko-yaki is strong and not too expensive. I'm never concerned about breaking it."

Yoshiko also noticed the small *furoshiki* he used as napkins, and decided on the spot that she, too, would employ this innovative use of the traditional wrapping cloth. Though it appeared he had gone to some considerable trouble, Carl insisted he was quite used to cooking for groups and really enjoyed doing it. Indeed, it seemed none of this was new to him, and Yoshiko marveled at the amount and variety of dishes he'd prepared and all the other things he'd done to set a proper table so beautifully, with such care and attention. After that first time, they were happy to accept his invitations and felt comfortable that they were not imposing.

It had taken all the months from the time Yoshiko first met Carl in late spring until now to find out what she wanted to know about him. But now, as winter approached, she'd gotten the answers to her many questions.

Carl Rosen had been married. To a Japanese woman. They were divorced the year before he came to Takaizu. There were no children. His former wife, the owner of a cooking school, was now remarried. These were the facts, as he told them to her. In between the lines, and at the end of the sentences where the spaces were, she felt she could fill in the other parts: that his heart had been broken, and that Carl Rosen had thought for a while he would never care about anything, or for anyone, again. That first year after the divorce he had to continuously remind himself he might still have a chance to have a good life.

He'd met his wife, Naoko, during his first trip to Japan. They were in high school at the time, and it was in her family that he'd been a homestay student for a year. And they both knew when the year was over that they would be together again. He'd been truly welcomed into the family's home. He was encouraged to call Naoko's parents mother and father, and they acted as though they'd lost a son when he returned to the United States after that first visit. When he arranged to come back to spend his junior year of college in Japan, they urged him to continue at his university in New York, sincerely believing it would be better for his academic career. When he insisted on returning, they became concerned. But they had no need to worry long. Naoko spoke up, saying it was her intention to marry Carl whether they gave their consent or not, adding without embarrassment, "We are already as married."

This pronouncement had sent her father into speechless shock and her mother into incessant talk of disowning her first child and only daughter. Her mother never forgave herself for being so unthinking as to let a young man into their home. In the end, they accepted the relationship, although they had bitterly opposed a marriage. It was an ugly business. It hurt Carl to hurt them, and he was glad when things settled into quiet resignation. Carl and Naoko were married, and though without the fanfare the parents would have wished and felt cheated of— "My only chance to see my daughter in a white wedding dress!" her mother wailed, crying real tears—it was pulled off without complete disruption within the family.

Naoko had been Carl's main introduction to Japanese, and to the language as a language of love. Although he'd always loved poetry, he never knew the beauty of feeling that could be expressed as Naoko taught him to express it in Japanese. Now, all these years later, he thought their love, its intensity, often expressed in haiku, had carried them away in a gentle passion. It hurt him to think she could be saying these same things to another man, that another man was saying them to her. Naoko was the first woman Carl had an intimate relationship with. They explored love as two young people will, as children who find a stretch of beach that had not been combed, a cave they think they've discovered themselves, and the belief they were the first people to enter it. Naoko was bold. The first time she padded into his room on bare feet, past the room where her parents and two younger brothers slept, Carl thought he was awake in a dream. Although at first hesitant, as Naoko stepped out of her sleeping robe and lowered herself into his futon, he could not reject the lovely body that pressed next to him. With only the thin walls separating his room from her parents, he didn't dare speak one word.

Years would pass, and she would, in the same bold manner, walk into their bedroom one night and tell him she loved another man and would be leaving Carl. Again, he was without words. He only watched as she let her robe fall to the floor and slipped into their bed, turned her back to him, and fell asleep.

8

A person could hear summer. A long, constant humming that seemed to rise from the ground and hang thick in the air. The very force of life could be felt in the multitude of creatures that crawled or took to the sky with small trembling wings. The summer burst upon them as soon as the rainy season was over. Nourished by the month-long rain, weeds crowded out all other growth and grew with uncontrollable forcefulness through cracks in the stone walk, and cracks in the old farmhouse too. The summer had been typically hot and humid, and though it was the end of the season, they could still expect at least a month of hot days. The really muggy weather and uncomfortable nights were past now, but still, the only time you could expect it to be pleasant were the very early hours before the sun came up. Once it was up, it was merciless.

No matter how early Chie got to the table in the morning, her father was already sitting there, sipping his first of what would be innumerable cups of *ocha*, green tea. She found herself looking at her father askance, wondering if he'd slept at all. Certainly, Mr. Uchida had never spent a morning in bed after six o'clock in his life, and now that might be five o'clock, or four.

Things had changed in Chie's family. Ever since Isao had announced his plans to marry, the very atmosphere in the house seemed to adjust to the news. It appeared their parents had realized overnight that their children were no longer children. There was no outward change, just a quiet mutual acknowledgment. Chie felt grateful to Isao for this. She had no intention of becoming one of those women who stayed young girls, with their husband's and parents' blessings, until they reached midlife. Although the whole country accepted young people as adults if they had reached the age of twenty by *Seijin'nohi,* Coming-of-Age Day, she hadn't really felt any different that cold January day, dressed up in a rented kimono and photographed at the shrine, but she felt it now. She wanted to be recognized for the woman she now felt she was.

The sun was just beginning to go down when Chie, lying on a straw mat in a small arbor built for kiwi fruit, put her book down. Like all farmers around them, the Uchidas had to try to diversify, and growing kiwi was one way to do it. Her father had balked, saying, "When Soichiro Uchida built this house, rice and tea fields were enough." The black-and-white funeral photograph of Soichiro Uchida, patriarchal in a formal kimono, looked at them every day from his honored place in the family altar. Tastes were changing, people didn't eat as much rice or drink as much tea, and Japanese now had a variety of choices of food and drink that the stern-looking Soichiro could not have imagined. Chie's father thought kiwi fruit was ugly, but had to admit it was an easy plant, needed little care, and yielded plentiful fruit. The three years before the plants bore fruit, he railed every summer at the leaves that covered the small arbor he and

Isao built, complaining the thick vines would choke off his other crops, though nothing else grew near it. And nothing could have gotten him to acknowledge that those same leaves and vines provided wonderfully cool shade, and the despised kiwi fruit arbor was the coolest place that could be found anywhere on their land during the summer.

The dark arbor was hardly fit for reading, but it was the one place Chie felt comfortable these days, where she could escape not just the heat, but the goings-on of her family. She could lie unseen for hours, reading until she dozed off, not waking until some insect had crawled over her. Once she woke just as a *mukade*, a poisonous centipede, was making its way up her bare leg. Using the edge of her book, she brushed it off quickly and deftly.

Hearing the five o'clock chime, she got up and walked to the path leading to the house. Catching sight of her mother in the darkness of the entranceway, Chie thought the woman looked older and more tired than usual. Mrs. Uchida and her husband hardly varied their regular working schedule, even in the hottest weather. Her mother's naturally dark skin was darker still from the daily outdoor work, the skin on her hands leather-like. She hardly looked like a woman who could have given birth to a daughter with Chie's fair complexion.

Chie would have been willing to help her in the fields, but her mother steadfastly refused, telling her it would be her "ruin" —ruin her complexion and her hands.

"You'll turn as brown as burdock," was her mother's way of telling Chie of the worst that could happen to her. Mrs. Uchida was convinced that these two things, a fine white complexion and soft hands, were Chie's tickets to a good marriage, and had told her so. When Chie answered she wouldn't have any man who judged her on such superficialities, her mother had given her a blank, uncomprehending look. Mrs. Uchida continued to leave the parasol by the door, and Chie continued to use just her sun hat. She was more concerned with having her hands free.

Isao entered the house just behind Chie.

"Oh, you're early today," she said.

"We met our quota today earlier than usual, and our uncle said we could all go home because it had been such a hot day."

"Well, that's a good thing he took notice. This heat is unbearable."

"It's been at least this hot every day this summer. I don't know why he noticed today," Isao said.

"And I don't know why you don't take your bicycle. It would save you time, and the downhill part would be cool."

"I know why I don't take it. I prefer walking to being mistaken for a high school student."

Isao didn't have a car yet and walked down to the bus every morning, and up the steep hill again in the evening. He'd passed his driver's license test and saved his entire salary toward a secondhand car. It would be one of those 500 cc cars that he'd described as "roller skates on wheels." After the wedding date was set, the first thing he and Tomomi decided was what kind of car he'd buy when they married. And this little car that he hadn't even bought yet was, in his mind, already traded in, or more likely, scrapped.

Isao sat on the bench-like step that led into the inner house and pulled off his boots. Sweat mixed with grime made it clear a bath was the first thing he'd do upon entering the house. No matter how sweltering the weather, no day ended without each of them in turn getting in the hot bath. In this weather, they'd cool down afterward by dousing with repeated buckets of tepid water, and then sit on the *engawa*, the veranda that circled the house. Their mother had already stoked up the wood fire–heated bath, and after welcoming her son home told him it was ready. Just a few months earlier it would have been unthinkable for her to offer the bath to her son before her husband. But Isao was considered a man now, given the same deference shown the older man.

Kimiko had come back to stay at her parents' house for the summer.

"She couldn't bear spending the summer in the city. She thought it was just too stifling."

Chie often heard pieces of news like this listening to her mother, whose phone voice was much louder than her usual voice. Chie knew her mother was speaking to the neighbor just below them, whose roof could be seen from their veranda.

"Of course, her parents had bought her an air conditioner as soon as the weather started to get warm, but Kimiko is not taking to being cooped up in a little apartment."

Continuing with her own commentary, Chie's mother went on: "She's a modern girl, but you can't overlook the fact that she's lived most of her life in a farmhouse. I remember when her grandmother was still alive and living with them. And her grandfather too. We have the mountains. And the river. No matter how hot it gets, you're cool when you have the mountains and the river. Naturally Kimiko wants to spend the summer at home," Mrs. Uchida stated with firm conviction.

Chie heard this news with dread, immediately thinking that

with Kimiko home for the summer, she'd hardly have time for reading. She knew Kimiko, hot and bored, would be bothering her, calling day and night.

Surprised, she found herself calling Kimiko first.

Neither one of them wanted to meet at their family's house, so they made a date to have lunch at a small shop near the station.

Chie stepped into the little shop, bowing her head as she passed under the shop *noren*, the doorway curtain. Kimiko was at the counter, talking with the owner, her voice, as always, too loud.

Greeting the owner, whom Chie also knew, she said, "Let's sit at a table."

There were only three tables to choose from, and she instinctively chose the one at the end. In a shop this small, Chie knew they could hardly talk without half their conversation being overheard, and as she settled herself in her seat, she wondered why they had chosen this shop. It was the lunch hour, and when another customer came into the shop just after her, Chie fervently wished the other seats would not be filled.

The owner's wife stood right behind Chie and Kimiko, waiting as they sat down, and then placed *oshibori*, cool wet towels, on the table. Chie picked hers up immediately and gratefully.

"Boy, you're sweating buckets." Kimiko watched Chie pat the towel on her face and around her neck.

"I bicycled." Chie held the little towel, now no longer cool, under her chin.

"I could have given you a ride."

"May I have another towel, please?" Chie asked the owner's wife after ordering.

Kimiko was not one to indulge in the national habit of talking about the weather and exchanging pleasantries before talking about what was on her mind, and when Chie felt cool enough to say, "It's hot," Kimiko shot back, "That's news?"

Chie just smiled, determined she would not pay attention to the fact that her light cotton dress was pasted to her back and armpits and stuck to the back of her thighs. Although she wore her hair up, wayward strands of her thick, straight hair lay in the sweat on her neck and were plastered to the side of her face. She would not let herself use a hand to brush them away. No, the weather didn't seem to be news to Kimiko, whose off-white linen dress appeared unaffected by the heat and humidity, and as fresh as when she'd put it on. She'd cut her hair at the beginning of summer, and now, trimmed even shorter, not even one hair was out of place. Chie hadn't cut her hair since junior high school: it would touch her waist if she let it down. Now she wondered why she hadn't cut it.

"I'm getting married," Kimiko said coolly, as if she had said "it's hot." She didn't blink, smile, or avert her gaze.

In an unconscious movement, Chie looked at the counter, at the owner and his waitress wife.

"Oh! To Kubota-san. That's incredible!"

"To who?"

"Kubota. Takayuki," Chie said, and not getting immediate recognition from Kimiko, added, "who does judo, right?"

"Oh, not him," Kimiko said, with complete disdain, as though she couldn't possibly imagine an intimate relationship with such a person.

"I thought you were seeing him." Chie tried to sound as casual as possible.

"I was more than 'seeing' him. Anyway, that was ended a long time ago. Just after I introduced you, in fact."

Kimiko took a cotton gauze handkerchief out of her straw purse and patted it lightly to her forehead. So she felt the heat after all.

"Besides, I wasn't in love with him. Now I'm in love," Kimiko said.

"Well, who? When?" Chie, hardly composed, looked at Kimiko in disbelief.

"His name is Kazuo Yoshibayashi. And I plan to be married a year and a half from now. If I can wait."

"Kimi, I hardly know what to say. What a surprise."

"You mean 'shock,' don't you?"

"Yeah, I guess. But really, congratulations. This is really news. What did your parents say?"

"They don't know yet."

Now *this* was a shock. Although Kimiko had always insisted on her independence, she was very attached to her parents, and they adored her, living, it often seemed, just to be of service to her. Chie could not imagine she would do anything to hurt or shame them.

"I'll tell them in due time." Kimiko took a small bite of her tempura and immediately blotted the oil from her lips with the small towel.

Certainly "due time" had come, Chie thought. Kimiko's parents would want to plan, make arrangements. It would be so much for them to look forward to.

They sat awhile as Kimiko told Chie about her plans, where she would hold the wedding, where they would go on their honeymoon, how much money she expected she could get from her parents and collect as gifts from relatives. Asked what she intended to do about school, she dismissed it as something that didn't matter, saying it would have to work around her plans. It was clearly not a priority.

"So. What have you been doing with yourself all summer?"

Whatever Chie had been doing certainly wasn't going to carry any weight or be of importance following this news. She hardly wanted to answer, "I've been reading," but she had nothing else to tell.

"Are you still taking that English class?" Kimiko asked. "A lot of people dropped out. I heard the assignments were too hard and that it was boring."

"No. I don't think so. Not if you like reading. And writing."

"I hate both. So, there's your answer." Kimiko sipped her tea. "But that teacher is sure handsome. He's kind of short for an American, but he's really good-looking."

"Yeah. I guess," was all Chie would supply in reply.

Kimiko took her little cosmetic bag and went to the bathroom, returning within minutes looking completely refreshed with freshly applied makeup.

Chie thought to follow her into the ladies' room to put on some lipstick but remembered she hadn't brought any.

"I've got to be going. I'm going to meet him." Kimiko placed her purse on the table, terminating their lunch. She tilted her head to the side, smiling the smile that made people call her "sweet." She picked up her purse and a small overnight bag and headed for the door.

9

K imiko was right about one thing, Chie thought. Carl Rosen was handsome. He didn't look anything like any of the movie stars she'd thought were handsome until now. But he was absolutely appealing. Sometimes she thought it might be his eye color, which matched the curiously colored suit he often wore, or that one eye appeared slightly higher, or lower, than the other. His thick hair fell in dark careless locks across an asymmetrical face. His nose was dramatic, dominating his face like a prominent statement. But more than his looks, Chie was comfortable around him. And it seemed enough to be around him for her to feel satisfied, fulfilled. It had taken time, but she'd come to relax during their regular sessions together when they went over classwork. Her English had not only improved, but also loosened up.

When she showed up at Carl Rosen's office for their regular weekly discussions, it occurred to her for the first time that it was odd that he, the newest member of the faculty, had the largest office in the English department. It was a spacious corner room with windows on two sides and sun from the south. All the other teachers' offices were so small that with just a desk, chair, and bookshelf they were cramped.

"It's nice you have the best room in the department," Chie said.

"There was a lottery to see who would get this room. I guess my luck was with me," Carl told her.

"I guess you are really lucky," Chie said.

"I took it as a good sign for coming to Takaizu," Carl said. "What do you think?"

"I guess you are really lucky," Chie said again.

As usual when he finished a discussion with Chie, Carl took a book from the tightly packed bookshelves that lined the walls of his office. Normally he'd choose a collection of short stories and tell her to read a particular one, and today was no different. Chie sat on the one spare chair, which reclined and had a small, worn footrest. Both the chair and footrest were shabby, probably had been discarded, and appeared to hardly belong to this room that was still new. Chie sat in the chair while Carl sat at his desk, working, and often she'd doze off while she read.

"Chie. Chie," Carl said.

She'd fallen asleep, and when she opened her eyes right into his, it was as if in a dream.

"I guess you're bored by Iris Murdoch," he said, turning away.

"No, no." Chie stretched out her legs and smoothed her skirt. "I love her story."

"That's how you show love?" His back was turned to her, but she knew he was smiling. She now knew his sense of humor. "I suppose if you only liked it, you'd fall into a coma!"

She'd fallen asleep listening to the soft scratching of his pencil, filling another notebook. He'd told her the soft 2B pencils were his favorite, making words "flow from head and heart to hand and paper." Watching now as he put his things in his bag, she was curious about what he did when he wasn't in school, but she never asked.

"You can sit here if you like, but I've got to go."

"No, I have to go to the library before it closes," she said, gathering her things together.

"Don't fall asleep in there. They might lock you up overnight!"

In the doorway she looked back once and could hear the clasp close on his leather bag. She wanted to tell him it would be impossible for her to ever fall asleep in the library, that the peace of being with him in the quiet office, a haven, cushioned by hundreds of books, is what made sleep possible.

"Goodbye, Professor Rosen."

The day had traded clouds for sunshine. Now, cool air settled on the evening.

As though she'd been waiting, Yoshiko opened the door as Carl came up the walkway.

"Am I late?" Carl asked.

"No. It's fine. Are you coming straight from the college?" Somehow, he didn't look dressed for school. There was nothing wrong with his clothes. They were just so different from the conservative suits her husband left the house in every day.

"Yes. I walked directly here."

"We can leave your bag here in the entranceway." She reached for the overstuffed bag.

"Are we coming back to the house?"

"I don't have a plan, but I thought if you want to have some tea. Or something . . ." Yoshiko let her words trail off into the indefinite. "But you don't want to take a briefcase to a jazz club."

After the first concert, Carl had asked her to let him know whenever there were any jazz performances. As concerts were few and far in between, Yoshiko made a point of checking the small clubs in Takaizu. She had never been to them herself but thought she could explore them in the company of Carl. Toshi begged off from this club-hopping, saying, "Count me out."

They walked along in an unrestrained silence until Carl said, "Did Toshi go to his mother's house with the kids?"

"Yes. They went early today because the children only had a half day of school. The sumo tournament is on, and both Toshi and his mother are fans. He couldn't get over there quick enough." This tournament they'd watch on television, but Mrs. Sakai was known to don her best kimono and go to *sumo basho*, no matter how far.

Mrs. Sakai lived in the same house Toshi had grown up in. It had been a new house when he was a boy, but now it was a postwar relic. He was the only son, his parents' only child, and after his father died two years earlier, Toshi tried to spend as much time as he could with his mother.

"Do you think she'll ever move in with you?" Carl asked Yoshiko. "Toshi said he'd wanted her to."

"No. I don't think so." Yoshiko turned to him as she added, "I wouldn't mind at all. But she likes being on her own. Or at least, she likes doing things as she's always done them."

Indeed, compromise, variation, and flexibility were anathema to Mrs. Sakai. Although Yoshiko knew her mother-in-law had a stubborn, narrow streak, and had at first objected to Toshi wanting to marry her, she felt accepted by her now, and she truly would not have minded if Mrs. Sakai lived with them. The comfortable room included for her when they built their house remained unoccupied and unused.

Toshi's mother was a proud woman whose pride had increased with every step up her husband took. He'd been an elementary school teacher when they married, and she had reached the heights when Mr. Sakai was appointed principal of the best high school in Takaizu ten years earlier. Although she now acted quite fond of her daughter-in-law and seemed to think Yoshiko was a good mother to her grandchildren, Yoshiko knew the older woman had no intention of being the second woman in the house, vying for the attention of her son.

"Anyway, it gives the children a place to go," Yoshiko said. "They can watch television as much as they want, eat everything I say they shouldn't, stay up as late as they like, and be loved even more for it."

"Don't you object?"

"Yes! But in a way, I think it's good for the kids. My parents aren't nearby. Toshi's mother's is a place they're always happy to go. They can be kids with no restrictions. It's only grandparents who can give them this. It's every child's fantasy, isn't it? I think it's good for kids to get away from their parents."

Her own parents had married late, and she never knew her grandparents. There had been no getting away from her mother and father.

Yoshiko led the way to the club, taking small streets and back alleys.

"What little charm this city has is in these few streets," Yoshiko said. "All the houses you see around here were built in the years just after the war. Takaizu was completely leveled during the war, from the center outwards. That's why it's such a jumbled-up, unexceptional kind of place. They started building, and no one asked any questions or had any plans or ideas. Just build."

"I really like walking on these back streets," Carl said.

"Well, I guess that's a good thing since these narrow lanes were never meant for a car to pass," Yoshiko said.

"I wish there were more areas like this," Carl said.

"What is true about Takaizu is true about every city in Japan from one end to the other: concrete, aluminum siding, block-like apartment units. Aesthetics concerned no one as houses were not so much built as assembled. They were shelter. Still, you can find beauty in Japan now but you must search for it," Yoshiko said.

"I'm glad you took this way," Carl said, stopping to look at a small wooden house, dark brown with age, topped with a gently sloping tile roof. Notably, instead of the cold bluish fluorescent light so commonly seen, soft incandescent lighting emanated from the interior. "I didn't know there were any houses like these here."

"Everyone loves the lake. But this part of Takaizu is my favorite," Yoshiko said.

"It'll be my favorite too," Carl said.

Yoshiko didn't bother to add she took the back streets to avoid the unwanted stares of passersby.

Soon they were in the downtown part of the city. What nightlife that existed was packed into the tight little bars crammed into small streets cluttered with signs, posters, electric poles, and overhead wires. This area was as bright and garish as the area they had just passed through was dark and somber.

"I can never figure out how these little places make a living," Carl said as they sat down at a small table just big enough for two glasses, an ashtray, and a red lamp.

"That's easy. Their customers come back. It's a matter of loyalty," Yoshiko said.

"Yeah, I suppose."

"Suppose? You always shop at the same vegetable shop, don't you?"

"That's because it's the closest."

"That's what you think."

Playing that night was a jazz trio.

"They could use a saxophone. Or a flute player. Or something," Carl said, sipping red wine that matched the music in mediocrity.

"You think you could stand a saxophone player in here? Certainly not a tenor," Yoshiko said, "and a soprano would be worse."

Carl's laughter joined Yoshiko's, with the hope of prolonging it. She rarely laughed.

"I guess you're right about that." He stretched his arms as though to touch both walls of the little club. "And this place doesn't get an A for acoustics, either."

Yoshiko asked for sake, but a club like this, caught somewhere between pretending to be a cool big-city jazz club or a French café, only had wine. One could choose a color, red or white, and that was it. Carl was on his second glass, wondering if he should order a third or just drink the one Yoshiko obviously wouldn't even taste. He reached over and took her glass out of her hands and poured it into his.

"You're a strange combination," he said, tipping the glass so every drop dripped into his glass. "Or at least an unlikely one."

"Why do you say that?" She put both hands around the empty glass he handed back to her.

"You know, the jazz, the flower arranging and calligraphy, the housewife. The rebel." He took a long sip.

Yoshiko lowered her head. Although the club was dark Carl could see she hadn't lowered her eyes—they were wide open and waiting for him to go on.

"Yoshiko. Tell me about yourself." She was the perfect housewife who ran the perfect home and was a model of traditional Japanese feminine grace, but Carl felt she had another side. He just wasn't sure if it was just beneath the surface or side by side.

"What's there to tell? You know everything about me."

"No, I don't. I want to know how you spend your day, every day. You can't be cooking and cleaning all the time."

"No."

"Do you read?"

"I don't like reading. I read enough at school. And besides, reading is for people who are afraid to live as the people in the books live."

"I wouldn't say that's true."

"No. You wouldn't. Still, wouldn't you say reading is a kind of escape?" Yoshiko now looked straight at him. She seemed to be gauging Carl, looking to see if the wine had taken effect on him.

Carl was silent. Unbidden, his thoughts went to Chie Uchida. It was obvious everything his student read was more exciting, more interesting, more compelling than her own life. Often, he found himself trying to imagine what the simple country life of this very intelligent girl could be like. And he thought, too, it might be a mistake to turn her into an intellectual, however unintentional. He had no doubt of her intelligence. He could tell it from her grasp of what she read and what she wrote.

But it wasn't necessary to think of Chie Uchida reading for escape. After Naoko had left him, during the few hours in the day when he wasn't gripped by total despair, he read. For hours on end, days on end. Sleep would come no other way.

"Yes, I suppose you're right," Carl said, coming back to the present. "It can be escape. But books can also be friends. They can save you."

The trio had stopped for a break. Every seat in the club was taken, and a soft murmur of voices filled in for the music in the tiny room. Carl had lost track of time and now wasn't sure if the band was between sets or if the playing was over.

"Yoshiko. Who are your friends?"

"You're my friend."

"Yes. I am."

10

Walking into the foyer of the old house, Yoshiko sensed the smell of a cat, as she always did in Toshi's mother's house, although the Sakais had never had a cat. There was something, just a little stale, old, musty about the place.

Toshi and his mother were seated in the small room where they always ate. He turned off the television program they were watching as soon as Yoshiko came in.

"I was this minute going to put lunch on the table," Mrs. Sakai said, standing.

"Oh, I'll help you," Yoshiko offered.

"No. You take a seat."

Yoshiko was just about to ask for the children when she saw them in the small garden that surrounded the house. The garden was dark with the boughs of old pine trees growing too close together, their trunks bent, branches twisted into desired shapes. Large rocks and stone lanterns kept the garden in shadow. The two old gardeners who came twice a year would pull out any flowers that had happened to take root in the garden as though they were the most obnoxious weeds. She saw Yoshinaga and Yui leaning over the little pond full of huge carp. When they were younger Yoshiko couldn't turn her back on them when they were out there. A garden mainly designed as a display of the family's prominence was not a garden for children to play in.

"So how was the concert?" Toshi asked.

"You do know it was a jazz club, not a concert hall, right?"

"Yeah. Did Carl enjoy it?"

"I think so. He seems to love music, and though he knows it wasn't the best, he still enjoyed it."

"He likes to go out too."

"Toshinaga said you went to hear music," the older woman said coming into the room, her arms held high and wide carrying a full tray. "With whom?"

"Carl Rosen. He's a friend from the college. An American," Toshi answered.

"Oh." After placing each dish carefully and precisely at its place, his mother went to the window that opened on the garden and said, "Children, lunch is ready." She added, "Your mother has returned."

Yoshiko was grateful Toshi had not only not objected to her friendship with Carl but encouraged it. She knew Toshi had always felt guilty about taking her away from Tokyo and the opportunities he was sure she would have eventually found. She had been so involved in the music world there that the idea of bringing her to Takaizu, a city that was culturally asleep, seemed unfair. Toshi often told her she should go out more and have more of a social and cultural life. But Yoshiko never complained and told him she was content and fulfilled in her role as a wife and mother.

When they'd met in Tokyo, Yoshiko was attending the best music college in the country. With the college's exceptionally small student body, every student felt they were stepping over the body of some other student who hadn't gotten in. But before she finished college, Yoshiko knew she wouldn't make a career in music. She had no idea of what instrument she wanted to play, let alone what kind of music. She couldn't accept anything less than passion in playing, and she felt she'd only been drawn to music because it had been thrust on her. For as long as she could remember she wished she knew who she was and what she wanted. She'd always felt she was what her parents wanted her to be. "I loved Mozart because that was what I had to play during my lessons. Although I've come to love jazz, I would never want to be a mediocre pianist," she'd told Toshi. And it was this fear that held her back from seeking self-realization in music. Like every other housewife she knew, she found the world of the home predictable and secure. She didn't need to be anyone else. She was a housewife; she'd never say "just a house-wife" because she knew what it is housewives do. And she was also safe in the knowledge that, because of Toshi's regard for her, he'd never tried to hold her back. She could be with him and, at the same time, be free. She had no thought that he would try to control her or prevent her from doing anything. And nothing meant more to her than her independence.

After lunch, as they sat around the table, she looked through the newspaper.

"Any other concerts on?" Toshi asked her.

"What?"

"Concerts."

She hadn't even noticed she had opened the entertainment section, and she quickly closed the paper.

Yoshiko was aware that the time she could spend with Carl had become all important to her. She planned everything around it—it was now what was foremost in her mind, always. She was happy Toshi didn't appear to be threatened by this relationship, and she often felt he pushed it. Perhaps it assuaged his guilt, she thought, because his mother demanded so much of his time. Mrs. Sakai didn't drive, and ever since Mr. Sakai died, Toshi took her on all her errands and to her regular doctor appointments for a slight heart condition.

"Carl is good company for you," Toshi said.

"Why do you say that?" Yoshiko asked.

"He has a lively intelligence, and his unending curiosity about Japan makes a perfect match for all your cultural and culinary knowledge."

"I'm not so knowledgeable, but I do like that he is so interested in Japanese culture in general."

"I have to say that I admire him. And during the seminar I got to know him better than a lot of people I've known a lot longer," Toshi said.

"You did seem really impressed by him," Yoshiko said.

"There is something about him that makes him so open and forthcoming. And Yoshiko, you know what impressed me most about him?"

"Please tell me."

"During the Japanese literature seminar, he never showed embarrassment if he were ignorant of some aspect of Japanese language or custom."

"He does seem really open to learning," Yoshiko said.

"He really is. I have to say that I, and all my colleagues, are quite practiced in the art of avoiding making any mistake in

English or exposing ignorance on any point in our fields. Carl made it appear to be the most natural thing in the world to say he didn't know something."

11

Tomomi came down from Aomori with her parents. After months of the parents deciding what would be the correct thing to do, Isao and Tomomi had taken the initiative. Isao convinced his parents it would be better for Tomomi's parents to come because, in addition to meeting the Uchidas (making only a passing reference to the fact they should be shown deference because of their age), the Hongos naturally would want to see their eldest daughter's future home. Meanwhile, Tomomi, who knew her parents had to be handled gingerly because of their puffed-up sense of self-importance as the largest apple growers in their area, emphasized how much they'd always wanted to visit Isao's part of the country. She helped them plan for the trip by suggesting what *omiyage* and *meibutsu*, souvenirs and regional specialties, they should be sure to buy for their relatives and nearest neighbors.

For the sake of convenience, the Hongos would stay at a hotel, and on the day after their arrival, both families met in the lobby before going to a restaurant in the hotel for a formal meal. Chie had never seen her mother so out of place before and wondered if this were the very first time she'd been in a hotel. Her mother looked strange—and strangely severe—in a new beige suit, and she now wished her mother had worn kimono. Her father didn't look quite as out of his element. Although he eschewed social gatherings, he often attended municipal meetings. On occasion he even had participated in campaigns of local politicians, and the dark navy suit he wore had been worn many times. Chie imagined he had been in hotels before—until he betrayed himself by bowing deeply to the doorman as they entered. Her mother, naturally, repeated this slip-up.

Although Chie had tried to get out of participating in this first meeting, saying something about only the principals involved needing to be there, her parents had insisted. After all, she was the *choujo*, eldest daughter. As the seventh person seated at the low table in the traditional Japanese restaurant where they'd reserved a room, she felt she was the odd person. The elders, assuming the young people would want to sit together, had placed her at the head of the table, with Isao to her right and Tomomi on the left. Gratefully, she found Tomomi open and friendly, with a country girl's easy warmth. Affectionately and respectfully, Tomomi referred to Chie as *oneesan*, elder sister, and actively engaged her in conversation, expressing admiration for everything Chie did. Speaking of Chie's "accomplishments," Tomomi "envied" that Chie could speak English, that she was so intelligent and attended college. Tomomi went on about how wonderful that Chie's skin was so clear, her hair so long and shiny, that she was so beautiful. Coming from Tomomi, these compliments didn't seem like empty flattery. Tomomi had Isao's open, generous nature and seemed to find joy in appreciating others, including Isao, which she did more with her eyes and with what she didn't say.

A three-hour meal in which elegant dishes were brought in one after the other by two kimono-clad women seemed to be over in no time. Although the two older couples appeared slow to lose their restraint and warm up to each other, the sake and beer (not touched by the women) soon lubricated their stiff exchanges. They'd spent the first minutes praising each other for their produce: the Uchidas insisting the box of apples the Hongos had sent prior to their arrival were the best they had ever eaten, indeed better, sweeter, and firmer than any that could be bought in this part of the country. The Hongos, for their part, were in raptures over the packages of tea the Uchidas had sent them, lamenting that their region's climate could not produce such fine green tea.

By nine o'clock the parents were all on their knees in the formal seiza position, their heads bowed on the tatami mats before them. Tomomi's parents insisted they could not allow the Uchidas to pay a bill that the Uchidas had prearranged to pay.

After their first meeting at the hotel, it was agreed they would go to a local hot spring the following day. Mrs. Uchida hadn't taken her annual trip during the Golden Week holidays, and the Hongos thought of the visit to the hot springs as one of the things they simply had to do. The area was not famous for its hot springs, but there were some good ones, and it would be a perfect place to get all the necessary souvenirs. Although it was possible to have had one large room as a family unit, it was clear it was too early for that kind of intimacy. The Hongos had a room and agreed for Tomomi to share a room with Chie. Isao could have stayed in his parents' room but declined, saying, "A grown man has to have a room to himself."

. . .

Contrary to her expectations, Chie enjoyed this time in the company of the two families. She'd made a point not to bring any books along so she could attempt to be sociable. If she had brought a book, she'd easily detach and end up being remote, vainly trying to reconcile the world of the novels she constantly read with the world she was living in. Now, no attempt was necessary since the very sociable Tomomi kept her engaged. In the communal bath, Tomomi scrubbed Chie's back, talking the whole while.

"You've such beautiful skin. What do you do? I've always wanted nice skin, but I guess I'm just too lazy to take care of it."

"Your skin is fine, Tomomi. You don't need to do anything."

When Tomomi stood up Chie could see she had the firm body of a farm girl. Her legs, thick from the ankles up, were like pillars for the full hips they supported. Her breasts were enormous.

They'd spent the day going in and out of the different baths, some claiming to soothe arthritis and others to heal rheumatism. All the baths had names, and Chie's favorite bath was "the Bath of the Dream Revealed," which opened on to a little garden of camellia and bamboo. Deeply relaxed from the bath, she was ready for sleep the minute she put her head on the hard buck-wheat husk pillow.

Almost half asleep, she hardly paid attention when Tomomi announced, "I'm going to take a little walk. It's so nice to be outside after the bath," and left the room in the cotton kimono all the inn guests wore.

Lying on the futon, now wide awake, Chie fervently wished she had brought a book. Her body seemed weightless after the bath, only her mind agitated her, and she fell in and out of sleep until, turning on her side, noticed the clock reporting it was past four in the morning. She noticed, too, in the still dark room illuminated by a half moon, the white sheets of Tomomi's empty futon.

"No!" Chie's mother said, her telephone voice hushed with disbelief. And then again, "No." Finally, "It can't be true," giving full weight to her denial. She talked a little more before hanging up. She paused for a moment as she passed the doorway where she could see Chie seated at the small table. Chie lifted her head from her book, expecting her mother to say something, but her mother just shuffled tiredly over to the sink. Chie looked at her for a minute, seeing the resignation huddled in her mother's shoulders and rounding her back as she leaned over the sink, scrubbing vegetables in cold water. Then Chie turned back to her book, lowering her head again in Eudora Welty's *The Golden Apples*. She slumped in her seat, trying to get back into the book, but now could only wonder what her mother had been talking on the phone about. Her no, incredulous, was also scandalized. For a moment Chie thought it might have to do with Isao and Tomomi. The thought made her blush, and she put it out of her head, pushing it to the far corners of her mind.

Chie didn't have to wait long to get a call.

"I told them," Kimiko said.

"Told who what? Your parents about wanting to get married?"

"That I am getting married," Kimiko said, her stubbornness on full display, "and that I'm quitting school."

"Kimi, you can't. The first year will soon be over, and in another year you'll be finished."

"I was only going so I could get married, and now I've accomplished that without having to bother to go through the whole stupid school thing."

"Oh, Kimi. Think about it. How can you?"

"You really don't understand, do you?" Kimiko's voice now took on a patronizing, condescending tone. It was as if she were talking to a child for whom she would have to draw everything clearly and plainly. "I'm in love, you know."

12

K imiko set her wedding for the end of February. Her one
and only concession to her parents was that she agreed
to marry on *Taian*, a good luck day.

The news had hit her parents hard. Naturally, they wanted
her to marry, but had no expectation of her getting married so
soon. They would've been happy if she received her junior
college certificate, which, for them, certified, foremost, that she
was indeed marriageable, thereby guaranteeing that the best
match could be hers. Still, they were quietly happy. They were
not dissatisfied with her choice of husband, and what they
desired most were grandchildren, and the sooner they could
have them, the happier they would be. It would have made them
happier still if Kimiko had chosen to live with them at home
with her husband. Their house was not big enough, but they
would have been glad to build an addition. After Kimiko's
grandparents died, it had been just the couple with their one
child, and when Kimiko moved out, they were the only family
on Uchida Road that was just a couple. All the households were
multiple-generational households, and they knew their neigh-

bors talked about them with pity. Kimiko, for her part, had never even considered living at home as a married woman, and as she told Chie, "It is out of the question." Her apartment would have been fine for a young couple, but Kimiko told her parents they could use the money they would spend for an addition as the down payment on an apartment she would buy.

Chie didn't know what to expect in Kimi's fiancé, but she liked Kazuo right away. At the end of the New Year holidays, he came to spend the day with the family, and Kimiko called Chie to say she had to come over right away. Chie changed her clothes and was over at Kimiko's house in a matter of minutes. She sat around with them eating *gyoza* dumplings Kimiko made. They were the one dish Kimiko could say she could make, and she wanted praise with every bite.

Kazuo, welcoming and affable, was the supervisor at a long-established construction firm and had attained that position while still young. He was thirty. At first Chie thought of that age as old, but now she thought of it as mature.

"So. What do you think?" Kimiko said after she saw Kazuo to the door. Chie tried to mask her discomfort about Kimiko taking a full ten minutes to say goodbye, during which quiet murmurings alternated with silence. And she wished Kimiko had bothered to reapply her lipstick before coming back into the room.

"Huh?"

"What do you think of my man?"

The last word jolted her, and Chie quickly regained her composure, hoping Kimiko hadn't noticed. "He seems very nice."

"Nice!" Kimiko plopped down on the cushion at the low table and took her lipstick out from the little makeup kit that was never far from her, applying the lipstick with annoying care. "How can you describe a man as 'nice'?"

"He also seems intelligent. And yes, he's handsome," Chie added as if in answer to a question. Kimiko had gone on at great length about how good-looking Kazuo was and would not show Chie a photograph, saying "I want you to see him in the flesh!" Kimiko had added, "He looks like the young Ken Takakura. Tough and handsome, all at the same time."

"Don't tell me he's not the most attractive man you've ever seen, Chie Uchida."

And as requested, Chie didn't tell her the most attractive man she had ever seen was Carl Rosen.

As winter flew by, Chie could hardly believe how busy life had become, between trying to keep up with her studies and her new role as Kimiko's bridesmaid.

When she ran into Carl Rosen after class one morning, he said, "Haven't seen much of you lately. Don't you want to sleep in my office anymore?"

Chie smiled faintly and mumbled something vague about having been busy with family matters. She didn't feel she could explain or reveal the extent of the demands laid on her by a friend.

Still, she hadn't fallen off her schoolwork, and continued to do all the reading plus writing assignments. Chie was thrilled when Carl returned one paper with his loopy handwriting in the margin: *You have gotten quite good at expressing yourself in English.* But she missed the afternoons she spent in his office while he did his own writing and corrected papers, and she dozed off in the chair like a cat.

Although Chie tried to get out of it, Kimiko insisted she needed her help in planning the wedding, the main requirements being that no corners should be cut, and the affair should be extravagant. Not concerned with the cost, Kimiko intended to include all the extra options the wedding palace offered.

The wedding day came and went. For Chie, it was an exhausting, trying affair. After the traditional ceremony at the Shinto shrine, the wedding party moved on to the wedding palace. The original wedding palace, which had been the largest building in Takaizu when they were still young girls, had disappeared, from one day to the next, it seemed. When the building was torn down to its foundations, many thought the palace had simply gone bankrupt because no one was willing to pay the exorbitant costs for elaborate weddings anymore. Certainly, none of the small shopkeepers and businesses in the immediate area lamented its demolition. The building had dwarfed every other structure in sight, robbing sun from their small back gardens. When a wedding was held, and there were always multiple weddings in progress simultaneously, the traffic jammed the narrow, normally quiet streets.

No one had imagined that the wedding palace was doing more business than it could handle, and when the foundation was laid for the new palace, and the great steel beams put in place, the locals viewed with disbelief the structure being erected in front of their eyes. Now the new, bigger, whiter, wider, taller wedding palace rose out of the street like an enormous monolith: eight stories high with fake Greek columns, complete with underground parking and a "chapel" attached. The chapel, with vinyl stick-on "stained glass" in a single long window, cross and spire planted on top, must have been a builder's comic book image of a church. The building in its entirety was a cruel anomaly among the older shops and houses that, although without distinction, held a Showa-era charm.

Kimiko sat at the head flower-festooned table, demure in her wedding kimono, her head bowed slightly low, presenting the proper position and mix of humility and innocence. She cried at the appropriate moment, when she and Kazuo walked past the guests seated at the many elaborately laid-out tables to hand bouquets of flowers to their parents. The wedding cake was cut on cue, with a large sword decorated with a white and gold ribbon hanging from the hilt. Stepping up to a microphone, family and friends delivered speeches with the right balance of good wishes and memories, humor and platitudes. Kimiko made several costume changes, going from the formal heavily brocade wedding kimono to a frothy white wedding gown, a pure confection of machine-made lace, ribbons, and satin-like polyester. Her later changes included a low-cut gown with red sequins, then a light turquoise dress with a train that was tied at the back in a large bow that trailed a good way behind her.

Kimiko made a serious effort to hide her outrage when she was made to wait her turn to have her photo taken with the white Rolls Royce (she had her choice of that or a shiny black London taxi) that all the wedding parties seemed to prefer. When their time came, Kazuo and Kimiko were photographed smiling in the back seat with a properly stiff chauffeur sitting at the wheel. If they wanted the car to move, that would've cost more.

13

It was no longer winter, but spring was still only a promise. A cool wind made it uncomfortable to sit outdoors even on sunny days, and inside the dark house it was too cold to relax. The heaters had been put away, and the floor brazier boarded up.

An unusual amount of rain for the time of year had first delayed and then robbed everyone of the full experience of the cherry blossoms. Their allure and dreamlike presence had come and gone before they could be fully enjoyed. It was reported on the radio and television, and when Chie heard her mother pick up the newspaper and let out a sad "what a shame," Chie knew it wasn't about war and upheaval in distant lands but the tragic reality of a spring beginning without a profusion of those delicate light pink blossoms that annually provided enchantment. While the entire nation seemed to mourn being denied the traditional cherry blossom viewing, in Chie's solitary walks in the woods behind the farmhouse she was delighted to see wild blossoming cherry trees standing in sharp relief against the dark boughs of cedar, cypress, and pine.

Things had quieted down a lot following Kimiko's wedding. Though Chie thought she would welcome the quiet and embrace the solitude, she found herself feeling deprived of the excitement and activity. Although it had been a tiresome bother, she now missed Kimiko's never-ending telephone calls. The school year had just ended, and although she looked forward to classes starting up in April, she felt overwhelmed with the thought she no longer knew what she was doing and what she would do a year from now when school was finished. She began to wonder why she had never really plotted out her future after graduation. While it had always been clear to her she would go into the English department of the junior college, she now thought it might have been smarter, certainly more practical, to have gone into the Commerce Department, or the school for early childhood education. A junior college diploma in English would not get her very far in the world of employment. She still wanted to read much more in English, but she realized she would always be able to do that, could do it anytime, on her own. Why hadn't she chosen to use this valuable time, time paid for by her hardworking parents, to acquire a skill? With a commercial certificate there would be no doubt that, with her English ability, she would be snapped up immediately upon graduation to work in an import-export office. An early childhood education diploma would have guaranteed she'd easily find a job with one of the many kindergartens in Takaizu.

Chie had thought going to college would settle things for her, help her see more clearly the direction of her life. But lately she felt things had become complicated. She wished fervently she could talk with someone, wished there were someone who could guide her at what she began to feel was a crossroads. The only person she thought she could talk to was

Isao, who was also easily the only person she trusted. She didn't think he'd have any advice, but she knew she could count on him listening.

Finding him alone in the kitchen gobbling a rice ball, Chie said, "I'm surprising Mother. I'm going to make dinner tonight. I'm making *okonomiyaki*," knowing this savory pancake was Isao's favorite and he could eat untold numbers of them.

"I'm going out. Getting together with the fellas to go bowling. Then we're going for okonomiyaki."

"Oh. I was sure you were going to be home this evening. It seems like ages since we just spent some time together."

Although Isao was as sweet and caring as ever, he'd become a shadow presence. When he wasn't at work, he was on the phone with Tomomi. Chie felt like he was a single man signing off.

"Yeah. It's been a while. But this is one of the few chances I'll have to be with the guys before the wedding."

"Yeah, you're right," Chie said. "You'll have a good time."

When her mother came in from the fields she was delighted Chie had prepared the meal.

"Too bad Isao will miss it. But I guess it's good he will have time with his friends before he marries," her mother said.

"It may really be one of the last times they can be together and they're all old friends," Chie said, trying to be understanding.

"Yes, they are good friends. But I'm grateful Isao was never like those boys who are so rough, particularly toward their mothers," her mother said. "I especially dislike when they refer to their mothers as *ofukuro*, as so many of our country boys do. They think it's clever, but it really means 'old bag.'"

"Isao would never say that," Chie said.

"No, he wouldn't. I think having you, an older sister, has had a softening effect on him."

Chie served her parents as she cooked the okonomiyaki on a hot plate at the table. Barely two words were exchanged as the three ate, and Chie lamented that if Isao had been there his appetite and enthusiasm for the okonomiyaki would have animated them all.

Now that it was decided Isao would marry in the summer, her parents settled into a quiet and complacent expectancy. It would have been out of character for them to be excited, and at any rate, what they had always expected, and hoped for—their son to marry and have a family—was now assured and need not cause them any anxiety. They were comfortable in their silence.

When Chie showed up in Carl Rosen's first class of the semester, he sensed that she was out of sorts. She didn't appear to be listening as she kept her head down and seemingly mindlessly twirled her long ponytail.

"In this course, 'British Women Writers, Past and Present,' we will first read selected excerpts of the work of Jane Austen, Charlotte Brontë, and George Eliot," Carl said. Noticing Chie kept her head lowered, he raised his voice when he said, "And in the second part we will read from the work of Virginia Woolf, Elizabeth Bowen, and Margaret Drabble."

After dismissing the class, Carl approached Chie as she moved to the door.

"They've assigned me a new assistant this year," Carl said. "What will be your school job?"

"Oh. This year I'll be working in the library. Stacking books."

"That's a nice job to have."

"Stacking books?"

"No. I mean in the library. Around books. You'll be the first to get to see all the new books that come in."

"Oh."

Carl looked at her a little longer than a passing moment, before asking, "Is everything all right?"

"Excuse me?"

"Are you okay?"

"Oh, yes."

She was obviously despondent, but he didn't want to probe, and as he held the door open for her, he thought how the bright red shirt she wore clashed with her pale skin and mood.

"I won't be giving any writing assignments for a while, but you're still welcome to read in my office if you like."

"Thank you."

"I have some new short story collections," he added, thinking it might tempt her as well as lift her spirits.

The minute Carl walked into his apartment the telephone rang. He put his hand on the receiver but didn't pick it up. He knew it was Yoshiko. She seemed to know exactly how long it took him to walk from school to his apartment, how many minutes it would take him to walk up the three flights of stairs. The phone rang for a long time. Long enough for him to take off his jacket, hang it up, sit down, and look at the clock on the cabinet where he kept cassette tapes and decide that it wasn't a good place for the clock to be.

It was almost five o'clock now, and he had about an hour of this light before the sun went down. The busy street opposite his window was usually crowded with young mothers standing around a small sandbox, chatting, before taking their protesting children inside for the evening, but he didn't hear anyone now, probably because the weather was cooler than it had been. But after successive days of rain, he wondered why they weren't outside. He smiled at himself, thinking how used to this place he'd become. If he didn't see the same man with the well-worn blue hat walking with his dog, a Shiba, at the same hour, he wondered about them too. The lives of these people seemed so orderly, quietly predictable, and unchanging. He found it fascinating that people could accept a life of such routine.

It wasn't that Carl didn't want to answer the telephone because he didn't want to talk to Yoshiko. He didn't want to make plans. And he was sure that would be why she was calling. He enjoyed all the entertainment she provided for him, but now he didn't want to hear her on the phone. These days when she called, she sounded breathless as she talked to him, excitedly telling him about another concert, an exhibit, a crafts demonstration, a viewing of temple treasures. If he saw her, he knew he'd see the sheen of perspiration on her forehead that always appeared with the intensity of her feelings. He knew he was the reason for it. When they'd had to cancel their cherry blossom viewing because of rain, Yoshiko had practically been in tears, and he was keenly aware that he, not the rain, was the source of that disappointment. He'd talked himself out of thinking he was in love with Yoshiko, but he knew his feeling for her was more than affection.

Carl sat motionless, staring at the empty space between him and the wall. He'd come to Takaizu hoping his light teaching schedule would leave him more time to write, but he had not come even close to producing a story a month as he'd planned, a goal he originally thought of as modest. One last deep orange ray of sun lit up the wall before dipping the room in darkness. Carl sat in his chair until the phone rang again. In the falling darkness he could just make out the clock: 5:20. He turned on the small table lamp next to the telephone, and then cut it off, looking at the phone without answering it. The ringing stopped sooner this time.

Surprising himself, he picked up the phone and dialed.

"Yoshiko."

"Carl? I just telephoned you not a minute ago. And about half an hour before that too."

"I know."

"What?"

"I wanted to be the one to call you."

Yoshiko pretended not to pay attention to this and told him the outdoor concert on the castle grounds had been canceled because of expected rain. The concert was going to be *gagaku*, traditional court music, which he didn't like.

"When will I see you?" he asked, not responding to the news of the cancellation.

"Well, I don't know. I don't know when the next—"

"Yoshiko, I will call you," he said and put the receiver slowly back in place.

Carl had let Yoshiko take over. She made all the calls, all the arrangements for their activities. That was just the practical aspect of it: she was taking responsibility for what was happening between them. He thought it unfair, and when he'd picked up the phone to call her, he'd made up his mind to share the responsibility.

He sat back in his chair with no more thought in his mind than whether he should turn on the lights or not. He thought about making himself something to eat, but he no longer had the desire to cook for himself. He had shared so many meals with Yoshiko and Toshi, either at their house or his, or at a restaurant, where good food mixed with talk and laughter, that cooking for just himself was now the last thing he wanted to do. He got up and instinctively walked to his cassette recorder and pushed the tape already in the deck. Soon he was enveloped in Coltrane's soulful "Ballads." He'd listened to this tape every evening now for a week. It fit his mood. Pulling the lever on the side of the reclining chair and pushing himself back, he thought Coltrane was better than food.

Now his thoughts drifted to the girl Chie, and he wondered what had come over her. How unlike herself she appeared today, worried and unhappy. In his mind he glimpsed her again in the clashing red shirt and involuntarily jerked in his chair—it had been that horribly incongruous. He thought she must not know herself, did not pay attention to her own feelings and emotional inner life. He could hardly imagine what could be wrong in the world of this young girl living in a secure situation with her family, and with her whole life before her. Soon the right young man would come along and marry her, they would have a family, and life would proceed with quiet predictability. If that's what she wanted. And in this moment, and for the first time, he realized that it might not be what she wanted.

Now, he pictured the well-dressed Yoshiko before him, also in red—a sunset red dress. She'd worn it at the last concert they went to, her dark glossy hair touching the shoulders of the dress in beautiful contrast, and he had marveled at the stylish woman before him.

"You look beautiful," he'd told her.

Her shy thank-you didn't match the urban, sophisticated

woman who stood before him. She'd changed incredibly in the few months since they'd met. Carl was convinced of this when they had again sat in the concert hall, thighs touching, and Yoshiko did not move.

"What's the matter?" Toshi asked Yoshiko when she walked back into the room.

"What?"

"Did you get Carl?"

"Oh. Yes. He'd just come in."

"You told him about the concert. I guess he was disappointed."

"No. I mean, I told him, but I don't think he was disappointed. I don't think he cares for court music."

"Good," Toshi said, and then seeing Yoshiko's puzzled look, "I mean good you won't be going out. We can have a nice quiet evening home together. Or maybe go out for sushi or something. Just the two of us."

He chose to ignore that she didn't respond to his suggestion but couldn't ignore that she looked drained and preoccupied.

Toshi turned on the television, distractedly changing channels before turning it off and asking, "Is everything all right?"

"I was up early making the children's obento for the school outing," Yoshiko said. Her tone was a perfect mix of frustration, annoyance, and surrender as she went on about what she "had" to make for their lunch.

"Yoshinaga only wants rice balls with umeboshi, but Yui refuses and will only have kombu seaweed." She told him the kids needed to take buckets and shovels and that she'd had to search for them in the outside storeroom. It turned into a housewife's lament as she ended up saying that they'd come back home with buckets of *asari* shellfish she knew none of them wanted to eat and, after trailing sand throughout the house, had left a pile of wet silty clothes in the bathroom.

"I had to go behind them with a vacuum cleaner just like I'm a *jochuu*," she said, using the old-fashion word for maid.

Yoshiko never complained about housework. Toshi could only look at her sympathetically, supposing the nervous edge he heard creeping into her voice now as if she were on the point of tears was a sign of exhaustion.

"You should get them to help out more," he said.

"I'm exhausted. I think I'll just get in the bath and go to bed."

"I'll come scrub your back."

"No, no. You just sit there," she said, looking back once as she started up the stairs. "Night."

Waking in the morning, the first thing Yoshiko heard was her mother-in-law's voice coming from their kitchen. Yoshiko always thought that considering how proper and correct Toshi's mother was in all her behavior and manners—sitting so erect it appeared a board had been placed in the obi of her kimono—for whatever reason, she'd never learned to modulate her voice. It was just a little too loud for a woman who always dressed in elegant kimono and sipped her tea from a cup held with two hands.

Yoshiko dressed quickly and went downstairs.

"I just got here. Toshinaga said you weren't feeling well so he had to make the breakfast. Are you better?"

"Mother. I said she was tired. I made breakfast because I like to do it."

"I'm feeling fine now, thank you," Yoshiko said. "Have the children eaten?"

"Yes, and let me get you something," Toshi said.

"You prepare to go, and I'll get her food," his mother said.

"No, thank you. I'm not hungry." Yoshiko rarely ate breakfast before doing morning chores like laundry and tidying up. She could hardly understand anyone wanting a cup of tea or coffee immediately upon waking, as Toshi always did.

"Very well then," the older woman said, looking at Yoshiko with a hard eye. "But I assure you, you are getting too thin. Of course, you want to watch your weight and not let yourself spread out. But it is not good to be just skin and bones either. Young women your age these days are avoiding rice. You must take in the proper balance of food."

"Yoshiko looks fine, Mother," Toshi said as he started up the stairs. "She doesn't need any of your nutrition lectures."

"I'll go change too," Yoshiko said, following Toshi. "I think I need to put on something a little warmer."

Toshi and his mother had planned to spend the day on the far side of the lake with the children. Yoshiko reentered the room just as the children came in complaining the outing wouldn't be any fun if it rained and they weren't able to collect more shellfish.

"Toshinaga said you were going to a concert again." The last word was said with just enough emphasis that made it plain her mother-in-law didn't approve. "With the young American man."

"Mother. He's not very young. It was an outdoor concert. It was canceled because of the rain."

"Oh, I see." She glanced at the window. "So, I suppose Yoshiko is free to join us now. I'll call and ask to have another seat reserved at the restaurant."

"I hope it's no trouble," Yoshiko said.

"Of course not," Toshi said.

"Well, you know, even though it's raining, many people enjoy the view from the restaurant just the same. I'm sure they will be full today as always," his mother said.

The children, bored as soon as they finished their lunch, ran off to the store full of toys, games, and snacks in the hotel restaurant's lobby to spend the money their grandmother had given them for that purpose.

The restaurant was mostly empty, and Yoshiko enjoyed the quiet and serenity suggested by the restaurant's traditional decor. She was glad she'd come, to be together with Toshi and the children.

"So. You get along so well with the American man," the older woman said. She'd moved the toothpick holder closer to her. Her habit of performing her dental hygiene at the table, albeit behind a well-placed hand, was another example of what Yoshiko saw as her mother-in-law's coarse streak. "Is he so interesting?" she asked Yoshiko.

"His name is Carl, Mother. Carl Rosen."

"Carl Rosen?" she asked, incapable of pronouncing the first name. "What kind of name is that?"

"An American name. That's what kind of name."

Yoshiko had mumbled something but not answered. She

was thankful to have the excuse of the glass of *ume-shu*, plum wine, she'd had with lunch as an explanation for the rose hue she knew tinted her face.

Rather than taking the more direct route home, they drove around the lake's perimeter. Yoshiko was happy to sit in the back with the children as they napped. Yui's head lay heavily in her lap while Yoshinaga leaned against her shoulder. She tilted her head on the back of the seat, and though her eyes were closed, she was anything but asleep.

Her relationship with Toshinaga's mother seemed to be built on contradictions. When they married, his mother had encouraged her to continue to pursue her outside interests, telling her, "Whatever brings you satisfaction, guard as precious." But then, she seemed to be resentful if Yoshiko pursued anything outside her role as a wife. Visiting them two weeks after Yoshinaga's birth, her mother-in-law had barely peeked at the baby when she announced, "Looks exactly like his grandfather. The Sakai family all have prominent brows." She declined to hold Yoshinaga, fearing to soil her kimono, and after a visit of an hour, slipped her small feet into her zori and, already at the door, said, "You don't have to nurse them forever, you know. I nursed Toshinaga for exactly three months. I checked the calendar. He's fine."

Toshi had told Yoshiko his mother was a "spoiled selfish woman" who did only what was absolutely required of her. If anything, he thought she'd been neglectful as a mother, and a wife, though his father never complained.

Yoshiko would have admitted that she spent far too many afternoons watching television melodramas. These were obviously designed for bored housewives, though she thought herself above membership in such a group. On occasion she'd turn on the television mischievously, just to know what kinds of things the other women were watching and thinking about. She didn't like the "drama" programs, knowing they were so evidently targeting women, manipulating their thoughts and emotions on the shallowest premises. There was hardly ever a character of a woman she could admire or even appreciate. A recent television program she'd seen she found detestable. This show had told the story of a calculating woman who stole her best friend's husband, but in order to live with him she would have to give up her own children. There were three young children, and Yoshiko was certain the program's producers must have gone out of their way to get the most adorable three children in existence in all of Japan. Adorable or not, Yoshiko was certain no mother would have left those children for the love of a man. Any man. But this woman did. Just thinking of it again gave Yoshiko a chill of loathing.

"Are you okay?" Toshi asked, glancing at her in the rearview mirror.

"Yes. Fine. I was just startled in my sleep."

14

"Oh, you've come," Carl said, answering the timid knock on his office door. As Chie followed him back into the room, she heard him say, "I thought I'd seen the last of you."

It had been her habit, and as he'd instructed her, to just knock and walk in. If he were writing he wouldn't stop, even to acknowledge her, but he noted if she took a book out of her bag or off the shelf. There would be an almost imperceptible squeak he'd hear as she settled back in the chair. He waited for it, and once he heard it, he'd go on with his writing.

"Have you been busy in the library?" he asked after fifteen minutes of silence.

"Not so much."

"So," Carl said as he pushed himself back in his chair, swiveled around to look at her, casually letting his legs sprawl.

"I thought I'd borrow the new short stories you said you have," she said, seeming to remember why she'd come to his room.

"When you didn't come, I took them home. But I've finished them. You can walk home with me and pick them up." Before she could answer he said, "I'll bring them in tomorrow. For sure. I won't forget."

On the street before he got to his apartment, he saw the man with the blue hat walking his dog, and they nodded to each other as always. The women in the grocery greeted him as he passed, the young mothers at the sandbox acknowledged him. He hated to think what any of them would have said, or rather, thought, if they'd seen him walking toward his apartment with Chie. They couldn't have greeted him and would have expertly avoided any indication of having even seen him. He chided himself for being careless, before smiling inwardly, realizing Chie would never have accompanied him to his apartment.

Entering her house, Chie saw Isao's bag by the door and remembered he was going to visit Tomomi. It would be the last time before the wedding. It was a long trip just for a weekend, but some problems had arisen, and it was a way of appeasing Tomomi's parents.

Apparently, they'd had misgivings about giving their blessing for Tomomi to marry and leave the family home. Originally their idea had been for her to marry and to adopt her husband into the family. He'd change his name to Hongo, and their lineage would be firmly established. They'd complained to Tomomi that it should be the husband of Chie who should marry into the Uchida household, since she was the eldest. They were convinced to capitulate only by Tomomi saying that no one, least of all Mr. and Mrs. Uchida, knew when that day would come, and that, confidentially, there was no reason to believe it would happen anytime soon, if ever. Tomomi was skillful in convincing them that they were fortunate in that they had two other suitable daughters, whom they could surely expect to marry well, and there could be no doubt that the first of them to marry would bring a man into the household, as everyone knew there would never be any shortage of available men honored to take the name Hongo and to eventually become head of such a well-established family. Finally, and this sealed it for them, Mr. and Mrs. Hongo, being considerably younger than the Uchidas, could stand to wait. It need not even be mentioned that they were in robust health and had many working years still before them—though of course their larger and more successful farm could afford to hire workers eager to be part of their agricultural enterprise.

Isao came down the stairs and seeing Chie said, "I'll see you on Monday. I've got to rush to catch the train." He ran out the door, waving back as his mother bowed. He yelled out, "Oh, Kimiko called and said she'll call back." He swung his bag over his shoulder and broke into a jog as he shouted, "See you!" before disappearing down the road.

According to Kimiko, in her long telephone conversation later that evening, marriage was "just bliss." She never imagined she would ever be so happy, ever feel so "fulfilled." Kazuo was "everything a woman could want in a man." It felt good to be "truly independent" of her parents (not mentioning she still accepted a generous monthly allowance from them) and have her own home. She felt now that the years before living with Kazuo had been "wasted" on pointless diversions and that now she knew the only "true happiness women live for: loving a man."

Knowing Kimiko, Chie listened to her with a measure of

skepticism but not without a measure of envy mixed in. She felt that all her life she'd been resisting Kimiko and her enthusiasms and, as a result, covering up her own feelings. She had those feelings, too, maybe not in the same proportions as Kimiko, who never seemed to think of anything else. Chie wanted to blurt into the phone that she, too, longed to "know a man as a woman," to feel "fulfilled," to feel she was not chasing after foolish dreams. She wanted to have things settled and not feel the confusion that most often disturbed her inner life these days. But she didn't say any of this to Kimiko. Not because she was talking on the phone in the entranceway and her mother and father were barely meters away in the main room, but because nothing would have induced her to tell Kimiko her innermost thoughts.

"That's wonderful, Kimi. I'm so happy for you," she said into the black receiver.

Carl left a small packet of books for Chie in front of his office, with a scribbled note saying he'd had to leave early and hoped she'd enjoy the stories. Unlocking his office door the following day, he recognized the proper penmanship of Chie Uchida on the envelope wedged in the door. He dropped his briefcase, mail, and the bundle of books he was carrying onto his chair.

Dear Professor Rosen,

I would like to share with you my true feelings. Recently I realized I am the most happy when I am with you. Especially when we are alone in your office, I feel comfortable and quiet inside. It is the only time I do not feel confused. I know now that feeling comes from love. I know now that I love you. And I hope that you will love me too. I am sorry to bother you because I know you are busy, but I must tell you this. And I tell you again. I love you.

Sincerely,
Chie Uchida

Carl's first feeling was of empathy. He knew she must have agonized over every word before she wrote this note. He knew her writing well enough now to see where she had hesitated, and that she had just "opted" for the "direct approach." He wanted to smile in amusement at her addressing a love letter with the formal "Professor Rosen," for apologizing for bothering him, for signing both her first and last name. He'd recently read Kafka's love letters, in which Kafka explains his name had been "growing shorter" with his passion for his beloved Milena, until he'd lost it entirely and could now only sign "Thine."

Carl shook himself in reproof: *How can I be thinking of Kafka when I've got a young girl, my student, thinking she's in love with me?* He scooped up his mail from his chair in a heap, dropped it on his desk, and sat down. He folded the letter and put it back in the pale peach-colored envelope and placed it between the pages of a book in his briefcase. When he leaned back with the casual sprawl he usually assumed when he was thinking, his mind and thoughts were anything but casual. He reproached himself for letting her get too close to him. Although he was certain he had not led her on in any way and had not even a dream in his subconscious of seducing this young girl, he tried to remember if there had at any time been anything inappropriate in his actions to have misled her. Coming up with nothing other than the incident the week before when he'd suggested she pick up the books at his apartment, he was now doubly thankful he'd caught himself. No. At no time had there been any impropriety in his relationship with her. Of this he was certain. He had befriended her, an obviously intelligent student with a better-than-good command of English and a love of reading. His only desire was to guide her in her choice of reading. He felt, too, she might want to write one day herself, and he'd discussed with Toshi what Japanese literature he could introduce and recommend her to read.

Although he thought she might absent herself, a week later she was present at his regular Monday class. He noticed she did not seem embarrassed or behave unusually in any way. But their eyes never met once during the ninety-minute class, which was extended that day by ten minutes while he explained the procedures to follow with the new equipment in the language lab.

When Chie knocked on the door and walked into his office as she had always done, he hesitated a moment before swiveling around in his chair. He stood up immediately.

"Thank you for the books." Chie advanced into the room and handed over the packet in the same wrapper he'd put it in.

"You're welcome." He took them, turned away just long enough to place them on the desk, and faced her again.

"I know you received my letter." Not even a hint of a blush tinted her fair skin.

How very brave she was, Carl thought. There must be a lot of courage and strength beneath the clear skin and modest eyes.

It was just an observation, but now he saw her for the first time as a woman. A young woman to be sure, but not just the young girl, the student, he'd always perceived.

"Yes. I got your note," he said, not taking his eyes off her.

"What do you think?"

"What do I think?" He felt a surge of anger, and then reminded himself he was dealing with a young, confused girl who must have had no experience of intimate relationships. He doubted she'd ever had a boyfriend. He was certain she'd never been with a man. What must have gotten into her to make her send him a note like that? Whatever it was, he had no intention of investigating the origins of this infatuation.

"Chie." He motioned to the chair. "Uchida Chie. Please. Sit down."

He was not sure what he was going to say, but he knew he was going to speak to her in Japanese because he did not want there to be even a hint of misunderstanding. Speaking in the most formal Japanese, he intended to make it clear that there was not, and could not, be any intimate relationship between them.

"Please know that I am concerned about you from an academic and educational standpoint, and I wish to encourage and support you," Carl said.

"I know," Chie said.

"If I can be instrumental in helping you find work after graduation, or directing you in some other way, I would be more than happy to do so. I think you are both talented and diligent, and I am prepared to write you a letter of recommendation," Carl said.

"Maybe I want to have more than a letter of recommendation from you," Chie said.

"Chie, listen to me. I understand that as the end of your two years of college are approaching, you might be feeling anxiety and even have doubts about your future. But I know you are a capable person, and I want to assure you that you may find success in whatever you choose to undertake—and that undertaking might not be clear now," Carl said.

"I have no idea of what I can do. What future I might have," Chie said.

"Yes, that may be true. But you are a young person with your whole future before you. You have every reason to believe you will be both happy and successful, as well as fulfilled," Carl said in a voice meant to reassure.

"But I am not fulfilled. And I know I would be with you," Chie said.

Carl wanted to shake her and tell her she could not possibly know him if she ever thought he would take advantage of her, her naivete, her innocence.

"You think I'm innocent," she said, though he hadn't said that. "But I'm not. I could love you like a woman."

Carl was confounded. He didn't give her dime-store novels to read and could only wonder where this vocabulary, these ideas, were coming from. The one thing he was sure of was that he wanted them dispelled, and before she walked out of his office this day.

"I do not know what is making you say these things," he said, looking at her sitting with her hands folded in her lap over a neat flower-printed skirt. She could still pass for a high school girl, he thought, as she sat there professing the passion of a grown woman. That she was inexperienced, he had no doubt. He could tell, though he could not have said how he could tell.

"You don't love me. You don't think I could be loved like any other woman," Chie said, trying, but unable, to hold back the tears that had been resting on the edges of her eyelids.

His most immediate instincts were to hold her, to comfort her, to pat her on the back, to touch her, but surely he could do no such thing. He had no desire to hurt her. But he knew he would. It was inevitable. As he had been hurt. And as he would hurt others. But he would not hurt her more by leaving her with any doubt.

"No. I do not love you."

He couldn't. He loved another woman.

15

"Yoshiko. Have dinner with me," Carl begged into the phone.

"I'm sorry. I can't."

Having already calculated she'd be alone, he felt a twinge of self-loathing as he pleaded, "Yoshiko, please. I know the family is away."

Toshi had invited Carl to go with him to a sumo tournament out of town and mentioned that "Yoshiko would rather stay in the house by herself than sit through a sumo basho."

"Carl. How can I?" Yoshiko said, sounding helpless.

They'd always met in public, or in the company of Toshi and the children. The intimacy implied in her going to his apartment alone seemed to her an impossibility. And irresponsible.

"Just a few hours," Carl said. "An hour or two."

When she finally relented, he felt dizzy. She wouldn't come until eight, when it was certain to be dark.

Carl rushed home, stopping at his regular stores on the way, buying feverishly and not chatting. Happy to be selling his most expensive seafood, the fishmonger showed his usual big toothless smile and said, "You must be preparing a feast." The feast under preparation in Carl's head was changing from minute to minute. He bought scallops thinking he might serve them as ceviche, then decided they'd be better braised, or better yet, as sashimi. He knew Yoshiko loved his Sicilian *uni*, sea urchin pasta, and he planned to serve it with *ikura*, salmon roe.

He took the stairs two at a time, and the first thing he did upon entering his apartment was put two champagne glasses in the refrigerator. He was reminded that the last time they were together, they'd lifted their glasses in a toast he proposed for Toshi's birthday. With a few of Toshi's colleagues they'd been a group of six, but all sound and conversation seemed just a background hum as Carl had been aware only of Yoshiko's presence. The most memorable thing about the evening for Carl was that he could tell she was as uncomfortable as he was. Always meeting in public places, they'd never shared a word in private, but he was certain they shared a feeling of self-reproach—not for anything they'd done, but the risk of what they might do.

"Well, here I am," Yoshiko said, presenting herself at his door. "I'm starving. I never eat this late. I hope you made enough food."

"As always, I made too much." Carl laughed. "But I know you have an appetite that will do it justice."

Yoshiko was indeed ravenous and delighted with the fine meal he'd prepared for her.

"Who buys uni and ikura? Carl, your taste is much too extravagant."

"Nothing but the best for you."

"But you're not eating anything."

"I often lose my appetite when I cook. Anyway, it's a feast just to look at you." Carl put his fork down.

"But why are you staring at me? Am I eating too much?"

"No. Not at all."

"Then Carl, please stop staring. You're making me uncomfortable."

"I don't mean to. I just think you have the kind of beauty that should not be taken for granted. I don't want to look and then look away."

Yoshiko kept her head down, her eyes on her empty plate. She noted that the small lamp that was always by the telephone had been put on the table. She was grateful he hadn't lowered the lights or placed candles.

"Carl. Please know I have never been in any man's bed other than my husband's. After we were engaged." She felt she had to say this, had to tell him this.

Yoshiko let her eyes fall on the tablecloth, the napkins, the peppermill. She surveyed the apartment, all in an effort not to look at him. But whether she looked at him or not, she saw she'd come dangerously close to him. She had allowed a relationship to develop that she did not guide as carefully as she did all the other aspects of her life. She never left things up to chance, and it was not in her to act spontaneously. Everything she did was toward an end she always had clearly in mind. Having let this friendship go where it will, maybe she *had* guided the relationship. Maybe this, or the possibility of this, intimacy with another man, was just what she had been guiding their relationship toward.

Lifting her eyes without lifting her head and seeing his eyes were still on her, she looked back at her plate. Carl got up and sat on his small and too-low sofa, the only comfortable spot two people could sit together in the apartment.

"Yoshiko, come and sit with me."

She thought his voice had the same begging tone he'd used on the phone when he asked her to come to dinner. She hesitated at the table, then got up and sat next to him. The soft folds of the midnight blue dress she wore lay loosely on her body and fell away from her knees to just above her ankles. She sat up straight, placing her hands one on top of the other. She would have looked prim if she didn't look so stunningly beautiful.

Yoshiko looked at his hands, as she had on so many occasions. She could see Carl follow her eyes as he put his hands over hers, enveloping them. She felt her fingers tense and then relax as he lifted her hands from her knee and place them palm to palm with his. Now her whole body felt weightless, without temperature, and then, as she closed her eyes, she felt the warmth radiate through her.

In a few days the month-long rainy season would be declared officially over, and these last remaining days seemed unusually heavy. The air, laden with moisture, made everything dank and damp. It was not possible to feel fresh.

Yoshiko knew Carl was awake when she got up. She walked over to the chair, quiet in her stocking feet, and slipped on her jacket. Recalling his holding her hands in his the night before, she could still feel the warmth, the sensation. She wouldn't look at him until she turned at the door and said goodbye, once.

It was still dark, just before morning light broke, when Yoshiko left Carl's apartment. Although not raining, a light mist, *usu moya* they called it, dampened her hair. She hadn't taken her usual nightly bath, and now all she wanted was to take a shower the minute she reached home. Carl had offered to walk with her, but she refused. Besides for not wanting to draw attention, she wanted to be alone. It had been an unusual evening. She needed to contemplate what had occurred between them.

16

Isao's wedding came and went. This time Chie was little more than an observer. Although Tomomi's parents had wanted a large wedding befitting their position in their community, Isao and Tomomi prevailed and kept the ceremony simple. Still, both mothers appeared in formal black wedding kimono. The Hongos presided over everything and were positively stately as they received and then saw off departing guests. The two Hongo sisters were beautifully dressed in expensive kimono. They'd spent as much time at the beauty salon as their marrying sister, getting their hair done and their makeup applied by professionals. As the Hongos hoped, it was made clear and apparent to all that they had two more daughters ready for marriage.

Chie, who hadn't been able to produce even one tear at Kimiko's wedding, now found she couldn't keep her eyes dry. Awash in memories of Isao and herself as children, she could only think she was losing her little brother. Drinking more sake than she had ever in her life made her sentimental to the point of being maudlin.

"I'll be home soon," Isao whispered to her before leaving by train for his honeymoon. His smile dried her tears, and then they were wiped away altogether when she realized what she'd always known: Isao would be living at home with Tomomi. The newlyweds would occupy his room, literally on the other side of a thin wall from hers. Tears now banished, Chie realized she would soon be living with two married couples. She had to leave. It had never crossed her mind that she would or could leave her parents' home before she married. But now that the idea came to her, she was ready to act on it. Her mother especially would miss having her around, but with the easy assurance there would soon be grandchildren—Chie's departure wouldn't be hard for the parents to bear.

As the time to leave school loomed before her, Chie still couldn't say what she wanted to do. She only knew what she didn't want to do: work in a bank, or an office, or any of the other limited jobs open to young women with a diploma from a junior college. She dreaded even the thought of having to wear a neat little uniform (navy for fall and winter, light pink in spring and summer) and sit behind a little desk. She knew there would be no prospect of doing anything more than the job she'd been hired for, and of course, she'd be serving tea.

"Professor Rosen tells me you're his best student," Toshi said, beginning his interview with Chie for a pregraduation guidance session. He recalled only vaguely the young woman in front of him now from when she sat in on his Japanese literature class. Toshi couldn't imagine her as "the star of the class" that Carl had so enthusiastically talked about, telling Toshi he thought her education to this point had been negligent of Japanese writers and he didn't doubt she'd come to appreciate them. Toshi saw the simple, meek girl he spoke to now as no different from the many other young girls who passed through his classes and appreciated getting a passing grade and getting out.

"I don't know," Chie said, smiling faintly. "I just like English."

"Of course, you won't be able to do anything with English, not without a degree from a four-year university. And even then," he said, without bothering to finish his sentence.

"Yes, Professor Sakai. I know."

"Well. What would you like to do?" Toshi glanced up from perusing her records and really looked at her for the first time. Funny, he thought to himself, Carl had carried on about her "talents" without ever mentioning what a very pretty, well-proportioned girl she was. Of course, it would have been inappropriate in the extreme for Carl to comment on her looks, but this young woman was so striking that Toshi thought Carl might have mentioned it. Even just as an aside.

"I'm not sure. I don't know what I can do."

"Well, let's see if we can get you situated. I see you live in Yano. Would you be able to come into the city every day to work?"

"Yes."

"Can you drive?"

"Not yet," Chie answered, adding quickly, "but I intend to learn soon and get my license."

When Toshi suggested a clerical position, he was surprised she had such a negative reaction and objection to being an "office lady." When he'd told other girls, they grabbed at it as though the golden doors of opportunity and good fortune had just been opened to them. He wondered, and hoped it wasn't true, that Carl had filled her head with unattainable and impractical ideas about literature and writing.

"Let me think about it some more," Toshi said, closing her file, "and come to my office this same time next week."

"Thank you for your help, Professor Sakai." Chie stood and bowed, clearly anxious to get to the closed door.

On the drive home, Toshi thought about his meeting with Chie and knew he hadn't been much help. He had been distracted and could hardly feign interest in the future of a young girl whose life was already written in stone anyway. She would come off her high horse, he thought, take a clerical job, meet a young man in her office, marry, have two children, and stay at home.

And for all that women complained about their "lot," it didn't appear to Toshi to be so bad. The security of marriage and the happiness of running a household and fulfillment of raising a family seemed to him enough. Women didn't have to concern themselves with the job market as though they were so much salable goods. Nor was it their fate to endure the infighting and backstabbing of the university world. He was expected to publish, and publish more, anything at all, for arcane journals—the more references, citations, and footnotes, the better—and for no other purpose than academic pretense. It was a climb to get ahead, and by a set date, to make a mark in the world of academia. He had to prove himself as a professor and a man, and nothing was supposed to be more important, as his mother never tired of reminding him, than he be "a good provider."

For Toshi, Yoshiko was the embodiment of the perfect wife.

He knew she could have made a different life for herself, but she not only accepted with grace the role of housewife and mother, she dignified it. She never seemed to feel demeaned and must have been confident she could still do more if she wanted. Toshi had told her that now the children were bigger and at school most of the day she should use her creative abilities. "Being a mother and a good wife and making a home for us is the most creative thing I could ever do," she'd said, and meant it. She loathed the thought of taking up some vocation and being mediocre at it.

Toshi stopped first at his mother's house, and not believing she was in, used his key to open the front door, leaving the package he had for her on top of the *getabako*, shoe cabinet, in the entrance hall.

Just about to turn away, he saw his mother slide open a door at the far end of the hall. "Oh. I thought you said you would be out visiting today."

"I was. All my friends are so old, it is unusual for anyone to feel good for more than an hour or two at a time. Shima-san and I had lunch and then tea, and then she practically threw me out of her house."

"You're exaggerating. No one you know is so sick or old."

"How is Yoshiko? I telephoned earlier and she really didn't sound herself. But of course," the older woman said rubbing the base of her back, "it is not unusual for a woman to have depressions at this time of life. They say it starts after forty, but it seems to me thirty-five would be closer to the fact."

"Yoshiko is fine, Mother."

Toshi had expected to see Yoshiko in the garden that

bordered their lot when he pulled into his driveway. She'd told him in the morning she planned to trim the azalea bushes, but he could see nothing had been done. Not finding her in the kitchen, her prone figure startled him as he stepped into their bedroom. Although it was warm, she had the covers pulled up to her eyes.

"Yoshiko." He touched the blanket lightly.

"My goodness. What time is it?"

"After five."

She let out a strange sigh.

"Yoshiko. Are you all right?" Toshi asked, knowing he was asking her that often these days.

"I'm okay. Are the children home?"

"I don't see them, but they should be here any minute."

When she pulled back the blanket, he was surprised to see she was still in her sleeping robe. Yoshiko caught his glance in the closet mirror as he hung up his suit.

"I just didn't have the energy today." She wasn't defensive, but her voice, her tone, was something Toshi didn't recognize.

"Sure. That happens sometimes."

Yoshiko got up, dressed, and went into the kitchen.

"I can make dinner," Toshi said.

"I know you can," Yoshiko said, opening the refrigerator and announcing, "We have leftovers."

Toshi saw no reason to ask her what was wrong. It was obvious enough she wasn't herself, wasn't feeling well, and he didn't want to annoy her. He felt she had the right to private feelings. There was no point in pushing her to talk, no reason to push them into an argument.

When they sat down at the table, he talked with Yoshinaga and Yui as he always did. He'd read somewhere that the dinner table was a good place to stimulate children's intellectual curiosity, and he had made a habit of talking to the children about some current event that they knew nothing about and had no interest in. Rather than eliciting the "lively exchange of ideas" he hoped for, he got blank looks. Yoshiko could get them in animated talk simply by asking who won the soccer game or made some reference to the characters in a favorite manga. She'd told Toshi, "What's important is that they express themselves at all, and the subject doesn't have to be earthshaking events."

Yoshinaga and Yui, little more than a year apart in age, had grown up with the sibling closeness their parents, both of whom had been only children, hoped they'd have. Since their earliest years, their girl and boy games had been interchangeable, and they were surely each other's best friend. Now, indifferent to their parents' higher goals for communication, they were engaged in a conversation of their schoolyard goings-on. After the children excused themselves, their parents were left at the table with their own communication difficulties.

"Are you feeling better?"

"There was nothing wrong with me. I was just a little tired." Yoshiko stood up and started clearing the table. Toshi got up to help as he always did.

It was clear when they got in bed that sex was not going to happen that night. Toshi tried to engage Yoshiko in a little bedtime conversation.

"Carl," Toshi said, "told me he's going to Okinawa. He's got a friend on Ishigaki Island and plans to spend a good part of the vacation there. We've never been to Okinawa, or any of the other islands, and a trip of a week or so would be great. I think we can afford it." He knew his mother would definitely want to go, and he could count on her to help with expenses. She looked for ways to give them money. "What do you think?"

Yoshiko inched a little further toward the edge of her side of the bed.

"Yoshiko?"

Toshi leaned over and saw her close her eyes. He reached for the light.

The following morning Toshi didn't have to ask how Yoshiko she felt. As soon as she was awake, she announced in a cheery voice, "Oh, I feel good. I had a good sleep."

"Good," Toshi answered, though he'd had something of a fitful night himself.

"Do you have classes today?" Yoshiko asked.

"Classes are finished. But we have guidance sessions, which means I must guide about thirty young ladies on the preset course of their future lives."

"That sounds easy," Yoshiko said as she opened the curtains, filling the room with sunshine.

"It is easy. They will do just what I tell them to do. And most of them will end up happy too," Toshi said, thinking about the one girl, Chie Uchida, who presented a problem and whose happiness he didn't feel he could predict.

"I'm afraid I don't have any really great or exciting news for you," Toshi said while Chie settled herself on the stool next to his desk.

"Yes, Professor Sakai."

"The best I think you can do is work for an import-export firm. There are several medium-size companies in Takaizu. It won't be exciting, but at least you'll be able to use your English." He handed her some company brochures.

"Thank you," Chie said, managing a polite and stiff reply.

"I know it's not a great position, but you'll be able to answer the telephone in English, type occasional letters."

Chie kept her eyes on her lap as he shuffled papers on his desk.

"You can type, can't you?"

"Yes."

"Then there. It's settled."

"Yes," Chie replied again.

"I think it's a good job," Toshi said. "At least you won't have to work on a farm."

Now she looked up at him. For people like Toshi, teachers and professionals, farm work was lowly work—hard, unpleasant work with few rewards. Certainly not paid well, and all a person could expect after decades in the fields was a bent back.

"My parents are farmers. My brother will be a farmer."

"Yes. But it doesn't mean that you have to be one too." When she didn't say anything, he added, "Look. Professor Rosen said he'd like to talk to you also about your future plans. I don't think he's in his office now, but you should give him a call. I'm sure he has some good ideas."

"Professor Rosen, this is Chie Uchida calling."

"Chie. How are you?" Carl didn't wait for an answer. "I'm glad you called." And he now regretted telling her he would not use the honorific *san* with her first name because it was friendlier.

"Professor Sakai told me to call."

"Good, good. Yes. Look. I've got some ideas, things I'd like to explore. Will you be working in the library today?" He'd already decided that the first time they met after the last time should not be in his office. He was concerned it might recall that occasion and embarrass her.

They agreed to meet early in the afternoon after Chie finished her work. Carl got there two hours before their appointment and was absorbed in writing when Chie came in. Carl closed his notebook and pulled out a chair for her at the table where he was seated. He'd been on the verge of standing up but didn't want to appear too gallant, didn't want the demarcation lines of man and woman to be too clearly drawn between them. He reasoned that every interaction with her henceforth had to be calculated.

Without delaying, he launched into his idea of what Chie should do. He'd been thinking about her possibilities and felt she had true talent in writing and that it should not be wasted. He knew of a writing program in the United States, in Ohio. He was sure she could get in with a recommendation from him. Of course, it would be an expensive undertaking with the tuition, room and board, plus airfare, but she would be eligible for assistance, and there were various international organizations she could apply to for a scholarship. Besides the college in Ohio that he had in mind, he knew of writing programs at several other small colleges in Oregon, Maine, and Minnesota he could also suggest.

"I never thought about leaving Japan to study in another country."

"Yes. But this could be a good opportunity. You could develop your talent and widen your horizons."

"What do you mean by 'horizons'?"

"The life you have here is limited. Your possibilities are limited."

"You mean because I am just a farm girl? Like Professor Sakai said, that I might end up working on a farm. And that's the worst thing that could happen to a person."

"No. No. Not at all. I truly believe you have talent, and I would not like to see it go unrecognized. I think you have possibilities for a future you may not have realized or even thought about."

" I've thought about it," Chie barely whispered.

"Yes, maybe you have."

"Perhaps you would just like me to go away so you will not have to see me around or near you," Chie said.

Now Carl knew he needed to be firm and clear.

"Chie Uchida, I have only your best interest in mind. My concern for you is that of a teacher for his student. It has only been and will only ever be that."

While Chie might have mistaken his regard and openness to engage with her for romantic interest, Carl was sure after she left his office that he'd made it clear that there was no possibility of a relationship. He also felt confident she would eventually get over her infatuation with him—quite possibly, he thought, he was the first man to pay her any attention. But he couldn't help but wonder what the future might hold for her. Although he'd first assumed she would get married after graduation and start a family, everything about her did not appear to fit into that mold.

Carl knew the reality of her going abroad to study was only a distant possibility, maybe the idea was even a bit grandiose on his part, but he wanted her to consider it. He could understand her hesitation, that going to study in America might be too big of a leap, but it genuinely disturbed him that she might end up accepting a predefined role—just because it was not only expected, it was also preordained, as if written in stone.

As Carl prepared his papers and books to leave his office, he glanced at the international newspaper lying on his desk and saw a cover story of yet another women's strike, this time in England. These days, he noted, there was regular coverage of women marching, protesting, demanding change. He was aware Japan seemed to perennially trail behind other countries when it came to social change, but according to Yoshiko, women here, too, were challenging and upsetting the "do-things-as-they've-always-been-done" standpoint of Japanese society. For all their modesty, reserve, and acceptance of conventional roles, many capable women existed in Japan, and he liked to think Chie Uchida could be counted among them. Yoshiko certainly was.

As if on cue, Toshi came bursting into his office.

"Hey! I'm glad I got you before you went home. We're having a party and you have to come! It's for my thirty-seventh birthday. It's not a birthday party, mind you. It's just a celebration to ensure that nothing happens to me in this 'bad luck year.'"

"Take a seat, take a seat," Carl said. "I'm always happy to get together with your family. But let me check my schedule."

"This is an invitation you cannot refuse, my friend. My mother is inviting you. Once you meet her, you'll know what a great myth it is that Japan is a male-dominated society."

. . .

When Carl arrived at the house, Toshi was there to welcome him. "Come on in. You're right on time. Of course, we expected you too early, like everybody else around here."

It was Carl's first time to go to Toshi's mother's house, and he was a half hour early, but rather than go straight to the house, he had used up the extra time wandering around a small park nearby.

"It's a pleasure to meet you," Toshi's mother said. "You honor us with your presence."

"I am grateful for the invitation and thank you most sincerely for the consideration of welcoming me to your home," Carl responded, equally polite and formal.

"Of course, Toshinaga wanted to have you. And Yoshiko," the older woman said, bowing slightly to her right, "would not have thought it a party without you."

Yoshiko kept her head lowered, and Carl suspected he was the only one who saw the color rise to her face. Standing next to the older woman, who couldn't have been taller than her grand-daughter, Yoshiko appeared to Carl to be taller than he normally thought her.

"Do come in," Mrs. Sakai said, breaking the spell.

"Where are the children?" Carl asked, feeling it necessary to speak the minute he sat down.

"They get to skip this," Toshi said. "I'm just joking. They're watching television. You'll see them soon enough—as soon as they smell food."

"Do make yourself comfortable, Mr. Rosen," the elder Mrs. Sakai said. "This room may be a bit chilly. We use it so seldom."

She needn't have told him. The room was obviously one for receiving guests and had the cold, unused, un-homelike feel that such rooms always do. It was a "Western-style" room, which is to say that it was too full with uncomfortable, dark-wood furniture. The busy patterns of the heavy upholstery seemed to grab the very oxygen out of the air. The kitschy chandelier that lit the room did nothing to lighten the atmosphere.

"That is my late husband, Toshinaga's father," Mrs. Sakai said, nodding toward the black-framed, black-and-white photograph that had caught Carl's eye. "He died three years ago, after a long illness and much suffering. He had lung cancer. It was a hideous death."

"Mother. I am sure this is not party conversation."

"Well, where has Yoshiko got to? Have her come in to entertain Mr. Rosen."

Yoshiko had quickly disappeared into the kitchen after welcoming Carl, and now came in and sat down. Carl noticed immediately that she'd removed the white smock that protected her kimono. She took her seat next to her mother-in-law. Her rose pink kimono stood out in great contrast to the older woman's sedate gray. The fine silk of the kimono flowing over her body seemed as natural to her as wings on a butterfly.

"I see you admire kimono," Mrs. Sakai said.

"Carl is very cultured, Mother," Toshi put in. "He's attained a high level in *chanoyu,* tea ceremony."

"Oh really. Which school?"

"Urasenke."

"That's the same school Yoshiko has her certificate from," Mrs. Sakai said.

"Yes, I know."

"Oh, do you?"

Thankfully, dinner was served, and thankfully, in a *washitsu,* Japanese-style room. The good taste exhibited in this room of wood, straw, and paper was the exact opposite of the pretensions of the former room. In proposing the toast, the older woman went on at some length about the necessity for her son to look after his health and be generally careful in this bad luck year. She would pray, make an offering at the temple for him, and keep an eye on him, even as his father continues to watch over him, and his family, to protect his better interest and ensure his prosperity.

For Carl, this wonderful meal that had taken two women two days to prepare was trial by fire, and he was grateful for the presence of the children, who were more talkative than he usually found them, and whose conversational content was considerably lighter than the formality of the tone that had been set from the beginning of the evening.

The evening ended with Toshi and Carl practically having an argument about the future of Chie Uchida.

"You're a dreamer," Toshi told Carl with clear derision. "Your plan that she go to school in America is completely unrealistic."

"Toshi, perhaps you are afraid to dream," Carl said. "Afraid to think and consider possibilities that are not the norm, even a little."

"Norms should be respected," Toshi said, making it clear he'd taken offense.

This conversation was brought to an end when Mrs. Sakai said, "It is true, Toshinaga, you are conservative in your thinking, like your father. Still, I am sure you will both give your best consideration to the future of the young woman in question. However, this cannot concern all of us here tonight."

. . .

"Thanks for making the party a great success," Toshi said to Yoshiko as soon as they closed the door to their bedroom.

"What are you talking about?" Yoshiko said, folding the obi, the wide sash of the kimono, as she undressed. She knew right away he was being sarcastic, a manner he adopted when he wouldn't be direct. It annoyed her.

"About you not talking, that's what. You act like you don't know Carl when you know him well enough to have accompanied him countless times on your private dates. Don't tell me you don't talk when the two of you are alone."

"I don't like your tone. What are you saying? Both you and Carl seemed to have plenty to talk about, including the life of a young girl who has nothing to do with us. The children chattered on. And your mother, never at a loss for words, didn't let a moment pass without having something to say."

"Mother is talkative, as you know. And as for the young woman, she has plenty to do with me."

"Oh, does she? You both appear to have taken a special interest in her."

"It is my responsibility to guide our students. And that includes that young woman."

17

"Chie. You've got to come here immediately."

"Kimiko, what's wrong?" Chie said, completely unalarmed. What could it be now? She was used to her friend's melodramatics. "Can't you tell me on the phone?"

"No. I absolutely cannot. You must come here."

Chie sighed and mumbled her schedule to herself. She had to go for her guidance session again, and this was also the day she was registering for driving lessons. "I won't be able to get there before four o'clock."

"Four o'clock! I'll have to wait for you the whole day."

"Sorry, Kimi. Why don't you just tell me over the phone?"

"See you at four. And don't be late," Kimiko said, and hung up.

When Chie walked into Toshi's office, her lowered head and hunched shoulders signaled to him she'd lost her spark. The defiance and determination he had seen in her earlier was gone.

He assumed it was about her employment prospects and tried to reassure her. He knew what Carl had suggested and could barely conceal his disdain when he told her to forget such a foolish and idealistic plan. Speaking to her in Japanese, his words carried more weight and authority than Carl's. And those words made it clear that this was not even going to be a discussion, certainly not a disagreement. He meant her to do what he'd suggested. Part of the teachers' responsibility was to see that their students secured gainful employment before they left school. And even once they had graduated, the teacher would pay visits to the various companies where students had been placed, to show the college's appreciation and gratitude, as well as ensure the next crop of graduates would also be welcomed at that company. Toshi said the company he'd recommended was signing recruits the following week.

"It might not be the dream job you'd hoped for, but I assure you there is no shortage of equally qualified young women anxious to take up a position with that company. They are an old, established, and reputable firm."

"Yes, Professor Sakai."

"It would be smart to get there and get there early."

Toshi had other students to see that day, and he didn't mean to spend more time than necessary to convince this young woman that she needed to be levelheaded, and that the idea of seeking a career, academic or otherwise, in English literature was one of the more harebrained schemes he'd heard in a long time. He thought of himself as enlightened and egalitarian, but what he intentionally presented now was his domineering, authoritarian side. As a Japanese man, he'd been brought up to not only make his will known, but also to present it with the assurance it would be carried out. Toshi couldn't tell her half of what he was thinking about the very real limits of her prospects, because it was obvious it would break her heart. Spirit too.

"I will go to the company for the interview," Chie said, lifting her head, resigned. The healthy blush she always had disappeared, and now, slumped in her chair, she looked drained, defeated.

Toshi noted to himself she hardly seemed like the same young woman who had shown up in his office just a week before. That young woman had an inner strength that lay just below the surface. But he liked this softer, vulnerable Chie. This side of her, now revealed and contrasted with the ambitious side, was attractive to him. Her solid country-girl character, juxtaposed with the radiant complexion and eyes as clear as glass, stirred him in a way that was not familiar.

"You're doing the right thing," Toshi told her. "If your parents have any questions, you can tell them they can feel free to call me anytime."

As Toshi stood up to dismiss her, he told her she needn't worry about having to speak with Professor Rosen again on the matter of studying abroad.

"I've already spoken with him," Toshi said with finality.

After her meeting with Professor Sakai, Chie was sure her parents would not have questions about his proposal, and if they did, they would certainly never dream of calling him. Unassuming people who had no doubts about their humble standing in society, they would never in a lifetime think to address a college professor directly, certainly not to question him.

Professor Sakai was from a different world. Chie knew her parents would be reassured simply by the fact that her sensei had guided her and suggested the work she would now take up. And she had to reflect that not only would they have had a thousand questions if she'd decided to follow Carl's plans, but there would also have been no way for them to direct those questions to him. Sure, he could speak and understand Japanese perfectly, but her parents would hardly get past the fact he was a foreigner.

Seeing Professor Rosen hadn't been easy for Chie. And she knew he had tried to make it easy. He no longer looked in her eyes with the earnestness he always had before. He did not try to engage her. Everything about him in his attitude and demeanor toward her seemed to have changed—except his sincere interest in her well-being and education. He'd said goodbye to her, telling her to read the college brochures he'd given her. She had read them and found such terms as "individualized curricula" and "innovative approach" baffling. Ohio, Oregon, Maine, Minnesota sounded not just exotic, but alien.

She tried to put her declaration of love to Professor Rosen out of her head—and hoped desperately he hadn't mentioned it to Professor Sakai, though she knew he wouldn't. She was embarrassed just thinking about it and could not explain to herself what made her do it. But still she was convinced she had feelings of love for her teacher. A longing for love that was so deep as to cause her physical pain and mental anguish is what kept her awake throughout the night. When she'd gotten Kimiko's call in the morning, Chie's eyes felt dry and sandy from lack of sleep.

. . .

Walking into Kimiko's apartment, Chie was amazed to see that Kimiko's red-and-white theme had been completely replaced with black and white with a few concessions to gray here and there. The sudden change, and its pervasiveness, couldn't help but be noticed, but she decided not to ask what happened with the red-and-white stuff that had all been new and, according to Kimiko, "my colors." Chie knew Kimiko wouldn't think twice about putting it all out with the trash.

"Want some beer?" Kimiko asked, turning her back on Chie at the door, leaving her to follow her into the apartment.

"Sure," Chie said, seeing Kimiko was already drinking a beer.

As Chie pulled out a chair and sat down, Kimiko took a can from the refrigerator and put it on the table with a tall glass with black stripes.

"So," Kimiko said, and took a big gulp of her beer, "I'm pregnant."

"Kimi!" Chie shot up from her seat. "Oh, my goodness. That's wonderful!"

"Oh yeah? For who?"

"Oh, Kimi. This is great. What does Kazuo say? He must be so happy!"

"I haven't told him."

"Well, when are you expecting?"

"I'm not expecting."

"What?"

"You heard me. I'm not expecting to ruin my life. I've barely been married three months. I'm not going to be tied down with a baby sucking on a bottle all day. Definitely not sucking on me."

"But Kimi. You're married. This is the beginning of your starting a family. And it's the result of your love for Kazuo and his for you."

"Well, look who's talking. Miss Virgin. This pregnancy is the result of not being careful." She went on to decry that birth control pills were still illegal, and truly irate when she added, "Japan is so backward. It's 1971!"

"Oh, but I'm sure Kazuo will be so happy when you tell him."

"He'll never know. I've already decided to get an abortion, and I know where. I'll just need some help getting home from the clinic afterward. Can you help me?"

"Oh, Kimi. Please think about it."

"I've thought about it. Will you come with me or not?"

Summer approached with the promise it would be unpleasant. Usually this would have taken the form of high heat and unbearable humidity, but this summer would go down on record for its number of cool days and too much rain, resulting in the worst rice crop since the end of the war. For Chie, the months that could be called summer would be remembered as the ones in which she learned to drive and was almost killed on her first day out on the road with her instructor when a wayward truck from the opposite direction turned into the incoming lane without warning. Both she and the instructor knew she would pass the test easily when she swerved out of the way and hit the brakes with deftness and speed, both actions of which saved their lives.

Two days after Chie's graduation, Kimiko had the abortion.

Chie was depressed beyond words, and though Kimiko was hardly joyful, for her, once it was over, it was over. When Chie went into the recovery room, Kimiko said with all the firmness she was capable of, "I don't ever want to talk about it."

It couldn't have been a week later that Isao and Tomomi announced they were expecting their first child in early winter. Chie overheard countless telephone conversations between Tomomi and her mother deciding where the baby would be born. While it was customary and expected the daughter would do *sato-gaeri*, return to her parent's home when she gave birth, Tomomi's mother insisted Tomomi could not make the journey in her "condition" and with the winter in Aomori being so harsh. Tomomi's mother was completely deaf to the reasoning that women gave birth in Aomori winters all the time, and that Tomomi's "condition" would not be anything other than any other pregnant woman's. Not to mention the sturdy Tomomi looked as though she could part her massive legs and give birth in the snow. The mother insisted she would come to assist Tomomi, though it was clear that it could not be possible for Isao's mother-in-law to stay in the house, and that it would be pointless for her to come and stay in a "nearby hotel" since no such establishment, they assured her, existed. In the end, Tomomi was able to prevail by stating the commonsense fact that her mother could be no help if she weren't in the house, and for that to happen, Tomomi should return to her *jikka*, family home.

But all talk of birth was tempered by the fact that it had been revealed to everyone in the family but the principal, Mr. Uchida, that he had been diagnosed with liver cancer. He continued having his nightly sake and sashimi, ignoring the side effects of his various medications and treatments, and blamed the nausea on the quality of the sake. Because of his blurred vision, it was now hard for him to enjoy his favorite television program *Otoko wa Tsurai yo* (It's Tough Being a Man), prompting his family to turn off the television.

18

When Carl didn't hear from Chie, he assumed she wasn't interested in his idea. He bundled the college brochures and pamphlets he'd collected, wrapped a thick rubber band around them, and stuck them in an empty desk drawer with the thought he could as well throw them out. He knew the kind of student he could expect to see in the future and didn't expect he'd have another one like Chie Uchida. At the graduation ceremony, he'd caught her attention for just a minute as he stood in the receiving line with other faculty members as the students filed out of the college auditorium. She smiled just the faintest smile. Carl smiled in return, a warm smile of pleasure in her accomplishment. He pushed to the back of his mind the thought that flashed through his head that the demure young woman with the blush of youth still on her cheeks, wearing the long-sleeved *furisode* that signaled she was unmarried, a maiden, and the *hakama* that covered the lower half of the kimono in modesty, had come to him professing love and offering her body. No, he thought to himself, it would be better not to pursue his proposal about the American colleges. He shuddered inwardly remembering Toshi's intense aversion to the idea and vowed he'd never mention it to Toshi a second time for fear of setting him off again.

He wouldn't say that his relationship with Toshi had become strained, but he did have a sense that a barrier had risen between them. Aside from the disagreement about Chie, Carl thought perhaps he was leaning on Toshi too much, both for guidance in dealing with college bureaucracy, and generally in getting settled in Takaizu. And he knew he was far too dependent on the Sakai family for his social life. He hadn't seen Yoshiko since the party for Toshi, and though he longed to see her, he left her alone. He told himself his deep feeling for her made it unimportant to him whether they were together or not. He felt so close to her, heart, mind, and soul, he could overcome the need to be with her physically. But regardless of the intensity of his feelings—and yes, it was love—a brief note from Yoshiko made it clear she thought it better they let their relationship cool and keep a prudent distance. She didn't say it, but Carl thought Toshi might be suspicious. He knew Mrs. Sakai was.

And so, Carl found himself alone. Again. Sensing the loneliness as an all-enveloping shadow, he couldn't remember a time when he hadn't felt alone. At least that's the way it seemed.

His mother started the tradition. She was the first in what would become a long line of women he'd love who were incapable of returning that love. Vera Woods was a passionate woman who was most passionate about her own life. She left his father, a man whose name she would not take, whom she refused to speak of, the minute she felt she could be mobile after Carl's birth. As soon as he could speak, she taught Carl to call her by her name and to never say Mom. Vera Woods could be said to be around—that is, from time to time she would bring her body, always wrapped in shawls thick with the scent of patchouli, to the place where he was, but she never kept her body there for long. She accepted that the birth of her first and only child would slow her down, but she had no intention of letting it stop her. His mother dragged Carl around with her from town to town and state to state, moving in and out of motels, and apartments that were never home. She had a life "in the theater" she wanted to pursue, first as an actress, and later as a director. She hadn't been successful at either.

When his mother was around, wherever they went, the first thing she would do was take him to the nearest library and get him a library card. This ensured that his earliest memories were of sitting in little wooden chairs at a table in the library's children's section.

"He just loves to read," his mother would tell the librarian, even before he could read. "Would you be kind enough to show him some of the children's favorites?"

"Well, young man, just you come with me. I'd like to show you some very special picture books."

Neither Carl nor the librarian, always a woman, noticed when Vera Woods quietly slipped away.

For Carl, the world of books wasn't an alternate world, it was the only world. Librarians always directed him to the best books, and as he got older, he learned to ask, and trust, them. They didn't know they were guiding a young man and giving him an education through the books they recommended. By the time he was an adolescent, he'd read all the classics "young people" are "supposed" to read. With their frequent moves, every school Carl attended would be a new school. He was never anywhere long enough for a caring teacher to take notice of a boy who loved books.

For a time, Vera left him with her older sister, who took him in even as she protested she had no idea what to do with a child. His aunt, a woman whose own passion had been only for alcohol, tried to give it up to raise her nephew. She wasn't successful either.

When Carl was accepted at college as an early admission, he knew he'd made it: he had survived his childhood. And just in time. Vera Woods died suddenly of a stroke, a brain hemorrhage that literally knocked her off her feet, and the sixteen-year-old Carl hardly knew how he should feel. But he knew to call his aunt. He had her name and number in a small worn spiral-bound notebook his mother had put in his pocket years earlier, with the warning "Don't you ever lose this!" When he telephoned his aunt, his only thought was he hoped Vera's death would not delay his going to college.

After his aunt signed the necessary custody papers, she said, "I know you're a good smart boy and won't be any trouble to me."

After she kissed him on the cheek at the bus terminal, the faint stale smell of whiskey breath in the afternoon lingered. Just as with the smell of patchouli, he was glad to get away from it.

Now as a member of the Takaizu Junior College faculty, too often Carl found himself as the subject of the other professors' jests about the so-called advantages of his bachelor status. He knew their envy was a pretense, even if they didn't. Carl was certain that not even one of his jesting colleagues, if given the chance, would opt for his lonesome life. Sometimes he wondered if he would be able to remain in Japan as a kind of odd man out. Among his acquaintances at work, only Toshi knew he had ever been married, and they never talked about his ex-wife or divorce. Carl had firmly turned down offers to be "introduced" but more than a few times found himself revisiting the idea with the thought there could be worse ways to find a wife. He'd come to think the lowered expectations in an arranged marriage might help the marriage to survive. No nonsense about love and romance. Companionship and cooperation seemed to be the foundations these unions were built on.

Carl could not reconcile himself to the fact that what was normal for everyone else—marriage, family, children—appeared to elude him. He was at the center of his own paradox. He cherished quiet, the solitude for time to write, and he was writing now more than he had ever, but there was no dismissing what he felt was a hole at the center of his being. Unbidden, throughout any day, at any moment, he could be assailed with a sense of longing. He wanted desperately to cherish and be cherished. He wanted the love of a woman. He wished that woman was Yoshiko.

A month in Okinawa should have been refreshing and rejuvenating. Carl was glad to get away, and to such a beautiful place, but the beauty and scenery he remembered from his first visit years earlier were now difficult to locate. Beaches he'd recalled deserted were now ringed with sprawling hotels. The simple warm island people he remembered as welcoming had become hustling and wary.

Mariko, the friend he stayed with, and with whom he'd had an affair years earlier, had had her share of men and short-term relationships, and now wanted to take up with Carl where they'd left off. She was an attractive woman and warmhearted, but Carl could only feel sorry for her, as it was clear love had nothing to do with her interest in him: it was desperation. He could only hope that he, too, wouldn't become as desperate. He felt bad about leaving as suddenly as he did, but Mariko found him with his bags in the foyer the second morning of his stay. He said he was taking off for one of the remote islands to deep-sea dive. He knew she wouldn't remember that he hardly liked swimming and wouldn't dream of diving. Carl did go to one of the other islands but checked into a high-rise hotel and seldom left the room. It wasn't much of a vacation, but he did finish a story he was writing.

"So, you didn't want to go to Okinawa, Toshinaga tells me. Why?"

When Mrs. Sakai asked Yoshiko, she looked straight at her daughter-in-law. Being so direct was a rudeness in which the older woman could indulge. And her question was asked in a way it felt certain she had informed herself of the answer before she asked it.

"I think it would have been too expensive. And I am sure it would be crowded this time of year."

"You know I would have assisted with the expenses. And never mind about crowds. Japan is always crowded. The children would have loved it. As would have I."

"I'm sorry, Mother."

"It's more important to be considerate than sorry." Mrs. Sakai's measured words were meant to chasten.

When Yoshiko made no answer to this, the older woman went on.

"Selfishness is not attractive in a woman. Certainly not a mother. Or a wife." And now inserting the blade more firmly, "You should have learned by now to subordinate your desires."

Yoshiko took this as just another example of her mother-in-law's contradicting advice. Yoshiko wouldn't have called it hypocritical, but she never thought the older woman meant it when she had told Yoshiko years earlier to "protect your independence."

They were sitting in the central room of the old house, and usually Yoshiko liked the simplicity and openness of the room, but now she felt suffocated. It had been their habit since the children were babies to spend Saturday evenings there, and often they spent the night, staying in Toshi's childhood room, which had been kept like a museum. Yoshiko had missed out on these evenings with no regret when she and Carl were going out regularly to hear music, but lately she went to the old house every Saturday.

Going to prepare the bath, Yoshiko was able to excuse herself from her mother-in-law's harangue. From the far end of the house where the bath was, she could hear Toshi come in. She couldn't hear what they were saying, but she could tell from his mother's tone that she was scolding Toshi for coming in late. Stern, she issued these last words: "You're a man. Don't neglect your family."

· · ·

Yoshiko could not remember a time when their marriage had been as strained as it had been lately. When the children were still babies, *toshigo*, born one year apart and both in diapers at the same time, she sometimes thought she would crack under the drudgery of it all. If her mother had been nearby, she would have had help. But as the situation was, Mrs. Sakai was there but didn't offer help, and Yoshiko wouldn't ask, though Toshi urged her to. He said his mother couldn't ask because "she doesn't want to meddle"—seemingly oblivious to the fact that meddling was her chief pastime. And the last thing in the world Mrs. Sakai would have wanted was for Yoshiko's mother to come. It was unthinkable she would give up, or share, her position as the senior woman.

Now that it couldn't be blamed on the children, Yoshiko was certain she was the cause of the difficulty she and Toshi were having. She determined she must do her best to be a devoted wife. She was devoted, but she felt she had to be more demonstrative, and she had to prove her fondness and fidelity. Toshi had not accused her of being unfaithful. He didn't have to. Just the impression that he thought she might have been unfaithful was enough to make her miserable. And his mother's attitude toward her, which had never been warm, was now positively cold. And suspicious.

"Toshi. We thought we would order out—for sushi. Or gyoza. Which would you prefer?" Yoshiko asked.

Although she was in her mother-in-law's house, she wore an apron. She didn't usually do this, and Toshi's mother discouraged it, but Yoshiko needed to. The apron signaled that the woman who wore it was in charge. This small piece of cloth constituted part of a uniform of pride and authority. This evening they both wore aprons.

"Oh. What everyone else wants," Toshi said, indifferent.

How unalike they were. Yoshiko was particular about everything. It might be what cup she used for her coffee, and that changed if it were morning or afternoon. She seemed to always know exactly what she wanted to eat. If she wanted a bowl of rice and miso soup, she didn't want anything else. She made an excellent Bolognese sauce—it took hours to make—and when she wanted that, nothing else would do.

While the children yelled out "sushi!" Yoshiko urged Toshi to choose what he wanted.

"It really doesn't matter to me," he said, somewhat annoyed. "Can't you accept I really don't care?" And finally, "You choose."

Yoshiko thought if they had sushi then they could drink sake, which could help take the edge off things. Yes, she did usually plan everything, but this was more than that: she was calculating. Mrs. Sakai frowned on Yoshiko drinking alcohol of any kind—"ladies don't drink"—but Yoshiko would drink this evening anyway.

"Get what Yoshinaga and Yui want. And let's order right away or we will be waiting forever for the delivery. It is Saturday night, you know," his mother said to cheers of "yay!" from the children.

Yoshinaga and Yui always slept with their grandmother when they stayed over. It was a small tatami room near the kitchen, a room that might be used by a maid, though Mrs. Sakai had used it to do her sewing when her husband was still alive. Now she slept in it. There was barely room to lay down two futon, but the three of them slept in there snuggled like cubs. Toshi and Yoshiko slept in his room. They never made love when they slept there, both uncomfortable with the fact that the old house, with its *fusuma*, paper sliding doors, and open transoms, didn't give them privacy. They had never had sex any of the many times they occupied that room. But tonight, Yoshiko wanted it to be different. She was ready and tried to coax Toshi.

"No. They'll hear us."

"No, they won't," Yoshiko said.

And indeed, they wouldn't. The children and their grandmother were in a room at the opposite end of the one-story house. After their fill of sushi, television, and lingering in the hot bath, without a doubt they were all fast asleep. And Yoshiko, warm with the glow of the small amount of sake she had managed to drink surreptitiously, had a true need to reaffirm her love for her husband. She wrapped her thin arms around him, caressing with love wherever her hands touched. Toshi was turned toward her, and his breath, touched with just a bit of sake, was warm and sweet. Yoshiko didn't just hold him now but gripped him closely. Nothing, she hoped, would ever separate her from this warmth, this refuge. For just a second, she felt a deep sadness with the thought that death would surely one day separate them. But love and the moment reigned, and she gripped him harder.

"I'm exhausted," Toshi said, turning on his side in one move that took the covers with him.

Carl and Toshi walked to a corner Chinese restaurant where they regularly had lunch. Regularly, that is, when Carl was willing to leave the sanctuary of his room and join Toshi. Mostly Carl skipped lunch and stayed in his office until his afternoon classes or meetings. A couple of times he'd ordered out or eaten in the college cafeteria. Both poor choices, it was no deprivation not to eat.

"What do you hear from the student Chie?" Carl asked, as they shared a platter of spicy shrimp.

"Who?"

"Chie Uchida."

"Hear? Hear what? I assume she's settled in her job and doing fine." He closed the conversation on this student, adding, "Once they've got a job they're all right. No matter how much they may protest in the beginning. That girl may have shown some talent in English, but believe me, she was no different from the rest."

It disturbed Carl that Toshi could only see her as just another student. He couldn't believe Toshi didn't see and appreciate her exceptional ability. In truth, he thought Toshi was obtuse to lump this evidently bright and talented "girl" with all the others. He could hardly hide his dismay, and disappointment, with him. Carl wanted to reply he didn't believe him, and that she was different, and most especially, different from the rest. But he let it end there. Although he and Toshi got on well, as usual, and their relations were cordial and as friendly as they'd ever been, there was something different happening between them. Carl knew Japanese ways well enough to know that what wasn't being said, or even implied, did not mean that it was not the main subject.

During his lunch with Carl, Toshi did not mention, or even allude to the fact, that he had helped Chie find an apartment. She had told him just before graduation that she'd be moving to town, and he asked if she had already found a place. With her reply that she had not, he said he knew of a couple of places, though he could not guarantee any apartments were available. His father had owned some real estate in Takaizu, rental apartment buildings managed by a broker. The income from the rent, plus a high school principal's pension, had guaranteed his father's later years were free of financial concerns. His mother inherited it all.

Aside from thinking he might be helpful, he also hoped that finding Chie an apartment would somehow blunt her disillusionment and disappointment at not being able to study further. He knew she had no interest in the job she had taken, and he could not forget her look of disdain when he said she'd be able to "use English."

Toshi filled out the forms for the apartment. For one question he wrote that the apartment would be for a young single woman. Going over the forms, the realty agent offered: "Oh. I see. A relative of yours."

"Quite so."

19

Chie surprised herself she didn't hate the job. There was nothing about it that interested her, but acting as interpreter and translator for her supervisor, who was obviously impressed with her abilities, gave her satisfaction. He regularly told her he'd come to rely on her, appreciated that she didn't need to be told everything, and was a self-starter, and he praised her competence and intelligence. The navy-blue uniform—skirt and vest—she was required to wear didn't bother her, as she'd been wearing a uniform all of her school years before college. Chie didn't even mind serving tea. She felt it gave her a chance to be gracious.

The Kosugi Trading Company did business with an affiliate in Australia, and Chie made a point to learn something about the history and customs of the country. She looked up words and terms they used in Australia that were not familiar to her and was surprised there were so many. She was baffled by the major difference in the seasons between Japan and Australia and kept on her desk a chart she made so she knew that when it was summer in Australia, it was winter in Japan. She read some of the short stories of the Australian writer Christina Stead but found her novel *The Man Who Loved Children* too dark, and never finished it.

Twice now she'd been able to welcome visitors from the Australian affiliate and was happy to sit in on meetings, take notes, and interpret for her supervisor. On one occasion, the Australian visitor complimented her, saying he was grateful for her prompt responses to his queries, and marveled at how polite she was on the telephone. He went on to remark how happy he was to meet in person the "lovely lady" he'd spoken with numerous times.

"Sugiura-san," Mr. Cameron said, addressing her supervisor, "you must have Miss Uchida accompany you on your next trip to Sydney."

Sugiura-san only smiled and mumbled something that did not commit to anything. But Chie knew his silence and lack of affirmation had a clear message: it would not be possible for a young woman, an assistant, to go on an international business trip. She could not be expected to interact with men of position, her superiors.

She'd read about Australia, and it sounded intriguing to her, but with few self-expectations, it was unimaginable she would be invited to travel to such a place. She would have been more than willing, was indeed curious, but having no confidence, she could not have made the case for herself to be included in these business trips.

Chie liked living alone. She could admit to herself she was lonely, but having time to herself, space to herself, was freeing. She didn't like eating alone, but she got used to that too.

Her mother called regularly, concerned that Chie was not eating well. She was not much of a cook and didn't really care that much what she ate. When the telephone rang in the one-room apartment, Chie knew it was her mother. No one else called her. Kimiko would call only if she wanted something, and lately she seemed to have gotten everything she wanted and settled into her housewife's life. For Kimiko that meant shopping every day, whether for clothes or food, it didn't matter. What mattered was that she put on makeup and a nice outfit, and go to one of the three department stores in Takaizu. Although they were more expensive than the neighborhood supermarkets, she bought all her groceries in the department store shops. Kimiko also now had taken to visiting travel agencies and collecting travel brochures and pamphlets, though she never went anywhere.

"Hello, Uchida-san," said the male voice on the other end. "This is Sakai calling."

"Oh, Professor Sakai. Hello." She'd never spoken with him on the telephone and did not recognize his voice.

"I just thought I'd ask how you are doing. How is the job?"

"It's nice. Everyone is kind, and I am learning a lot. Mr. Sugiura, my supervisor, is very kind and helpful."

"I am pleased to hear it. And the apartment?"

"It is quite pleasant and satisfactory. Thank you again." Chie lamented the lack of closet space, which was insufficient even for the few clothes she had. But she would never have complained about it to him.

"Well, if you need anything, please let me know. I can speak with the building manager."

"Thank you, Professor Sakai."

When she hung up, Chie wondered how she would have let

him know anything. After she'd graduated, there was no possibility of her visiting him at the college. And she did not have his direct telephone number.

The new semester had begun, and although Carl did not see Toshi as often as he had when he first started teaching at the college, they did meet on occasion. Spotting Toshi in the hall, Carl stopped to chat for a minute and asked after the family.

"Oh, everyone's fine. Yoshinaga has entered junior high school. Now cram school begins in earnest. He is not at all interested, but Yoshiko has made it her life's work. Even after a relentless search for the best cram school, she doesn't stop looking in the event a better one might be out there. I didn't realize she was such a *kyoiku mama*. It seems to be the only thing that interests her these days."

"Oh really? But I guess it's wonderful she's such a conscientious mother, dedicated to her children's education."

"I guess so. She seems to be less interested in going out, music and all that stuff."

Carl noted that she had not invited him to any music events for months now. There wasn't anything he could really do or say about it. And he hadn't received any invitations from Toshi for quite a while now either. The kite festival was coming up, and though Carl knew Toshi never missed it, he didn't mention it. Carl just thought how the time had passed since the three of them had gone out happy, even merry, together. Now it seemed like ages ago, in a fantastical time.

"Well, the school year is off to a busy start. I am sure you, too, are up to your ears," Carl said, adding, "and there don't appear to be any particularly bright lights among this new crop of young ladies."

It was a clear, if not direct, reference to Chie Uchida.

"See you around, Carl."

"See you."

When Toshi reached his home that evening, he felt the distinct difference in the welcome he received. Not just from Yoshiko, but the children too. Yoshinaga, who had always been described as *akarui*, a cheerful child, now appeared always sullen. His head bent over his desk, his homework, his books. And there was *bukatsu*—he was compelled to be in the soccer sports club and did not like it at all.

Yoshiko was in the kitchen, preparing a meal. All their meals now seemed to be elaborate, as if that was all that mattered. She spoke of making sure Yoshinaga got enough calories, that he needed good food to make him energetic. Although she'd always hated making fried foods, now she was making them all the time. Typical Japanese meals, already plenty elaborate, were now enhanced with salads with countless ingredients and homemade dressings.

"Dinner will be ready in about fifteen minutes," Yoshiko said, forgetting even the customary *okaerinasai*, welcome home.

"*Tadaima*," Toshi said sarcastically, adding emphasis to this usual "I'm home."

"Oh. *Okaeri*. I just have to finish making the fry and then I'll set the table. I should make a salad too, but maybe this will be enough."

Toshi couldn't help but notice these days her speech was peppered with "have to" and "should," as if she did nothing from her own volition, and choice, anymore. She was obligated to do what she did.

They ate in silence. Toshi no longer bothered the children with questions about their day or anything else. He remembered he, too, had had a sullen, withdrawn period as an adolescent. But in his case, his home had hardly been the happy place he and Yoshiko earnestly strived to create for their children. As an only child, he'd often felt he was tolerated by his father, and all but neglected by his mother. She had no intention of being a playmate and was perfunctory in carrying out her maternal duties.

When Toshi showed up at Chie's apartment building the following Saturday morning, he hardly knew why he was there. He'd said he was going for a walk around the lake, and had ended up downtown, nowhere near the lake. Her curtains were drawn, but he felt certain he could see movement in the ground floor apartment. The building was old, the first one his father had bought. Located at the end of a street with no other buildings, and two old houses, he was unnoticed as he stood on the street outside. He thought about ringing her bell, but in the same moment could not imagine why he would ring her bell. If she'd come to the door, he would have been speechless. Retreating to a small coffee shop, he saw her pass by on the opposite side of the street, probably on her way to the station. He felt relief that she hadn't seen him. Never mind appearing at her door, he would not have been able to explain his reason for being in that area, a place he never went.

Regular Saturdays at his mother's were now not so regular. These days everything was arranged around Yoshinaga's schedule. Mrs. Sakai resented it because she thought everything should be arranged around her. And as for the family staying over, there could be no thought of her grandson sharing her bedroom anymore. The chattering Yui was company, but Mrs. Sakai, whose hearing was failing, felt her granddaughter was always whispering. She found it annoying.

"Where did you go? I thought you said you were walking at the lake. I figured you'd be back a lot sooner," Yoshiko said as Toshi came in.

"I decided to walk around town a bit."

"What?"

Toshi regretted what he said as an excuse for being late as soon as he'd said it. It was implausible that he'd "walk around town" and he knew it.

"I have to do some grocery shopping. Yoshinaga has a soccer tournament tomorrow and I've got to get some items for his obento. And his water bottle is leaking. I have to buy a new one."

Toshi wasn't listening.

Chie made an effort to spend the weekends with her parents, but she didn't feel as comfortable at home. After the birth of Isao and Tomomi's baby boy, Shohei, nothing and no one else seemed to matter. Chie was happiest for her mother, who appeared to get a new life with this new baby. The excitement and joy of the baby was unfolding on a backdrop of her father's deteriorating health. He had his sake on the table before him as he always did, lifted the glass to his lips but did not take a sip. His wife dutifully served up *otsumami*, but he no longer touched this favorite snack of chewy dried squid. Having lost his farmer's deep bronze coloring, Mr. Uchida appeared to be fading before their eyes as his skin had become an odd color of gray. His hair, once thick and dark, was now without luster, and the few remaining strands had turned completely white. The baby, robust with bright pink round cheeks and a shock of black hair, presented a sharp contrast.

How out of place Chie felt. There was nothing for her there. Although her mother appeared to dote on her as usual, it was Isao and Tomomi, and the baby Shohei, who were the true focus of all her attention. Chie, sitting alone in her room, was surprised she'd ever liked it. It really was a storeroom. She'd taken most of her things to her apartment, but the few items left —books, notebooks, school uniforms, a few stuffed animals, already dusty and moldy—stood as a sad reminder of her earlier life.

"Dear elder sister, we're so happy to have you home. You look so lovely as usual. Look at me, I am fatter than ever," Tomomi said.

"Tomomi, you look wonderful, healthy and happy. And just look at Shohei. He's gotten so much bigger even from when I saw him two weeks ago. And just look at those fat cheeks!"

"That's from nursing. It seems he can't get enough *oppai*, breastfeeding."

Chie didn't know how to respond to that and could only wonder what it would be like to have a baby, a person, sucking on your breast.

"Those cheeks are the best sign he's a healthy baby and getting all the nourishment he needs," Mrs. Uchida chimed in.

At dinner they all pretended to be interested in Chie's job, though none of them could understand or relate to what she was doing.

"Australia is so far away. Are they going to send you there?" Isao asked.

"No. I don't think it's likely I'll be going to Australia. Though I'd love to. I've read a lot about it, and it sounds like a wonderful country. And it's huge. It's probably a hundred times the size of Japan."

"Wow, really? So why don't you tell them you'd like to go? I mean, ask them."

"Isao, it doesn't work like that. I don't have the standing to be invited on an international business trip." And she added, "I'm still a new employee. A 'new grad.'"

"But you have the position to be doing all the talking for your boss. You should probably go instead of him," Isao said.

Yes, Chie thought that if she went, probably the trip would be more productive and worthwhile. Sugiura-san's managerial style indicated he thought holding long meetings was the same as working. Additionally, he wanted everything double-checked, produced in duplicate, officially stamped, and filed. Employees who were not concerned with the matter under discussion would receive summaries of the meetings and unwanted reports, papers piled upon papers, in their inboxes. Chie dutifully sat in on many of these meetings and was always amazed how little was accomplished. Often, she'd have a suggestion, but opinions were not asked for, and she knew it would not be welcome. Saying something, even as an idea, would probably be thought impertinent. If she dared to speak up, they might think her arrogant, even aggressive. As for Australia, there would never be an opportunity for her to even mention it. Now talking with Isao, she made up her mind never to suggest it and quickly changed the subject.

"Mother, how is Mrs. Kurokawa? Is she out of the hospital?"

"Oh yes. She's fine. Lucky her fall was only a broken wrist. They say a broken hip spells the end." *Netakiri*, confined to the bed, was what all these old people most feared. "Fortunately," her mother went on, "she has her eldest son at home still. But at the same time, it's not so fortunate he hasn't married yet."

"He's only a few years older than me. It is not exactly late for him not to have found a wife," Chie said.

"No one is talking about 'finding,' Chie. He needs to be introduced to someone suitable. Soon."

Chie didn't want to argue with her mother. She knew how people of her mother's generation thought. Marriage was an arrangement. The parents were the best placed to choose a mate. A deal had to be made. And as her mother said, the sooner the better. Sure, they had gone along with Isao marrying the woman of his choice, but that was to be seen as an exception, and they considered themselves lenient, even modern, that they had accepted it. For her parents, all talk of romance was foolish. Such a thing as "falling in love" sounded ridiculous.

"I hope she'll be feeling better. Please give her my best regards," Chie said.

"You can give them yourself. She's coming over tomorrow in the afternoon to see the baby. Takashi will drive her," Mrs. Uchida said.

"Mother. You can see their roof from our house. Why would she need to be driven?"

"She says ever since her fall she doesn't feel steady on her feet. And since Takashi is at home, he can perform this small service for his aging mother."

"I'll be leaving early." Chie didn't mind coming home, but she had no intention of interacting with neighbors.

"Chie, you must stay. It is ages since you've seen Mrs. Kurokawa. I know she'd be happy to see you. It will give her some cheer."

Playing the role of the elder daughter home for a visit, Chie hung around until Mrs. Kurokawa showed up bearing a gift of a large bag of dried shiitake, though the Uchidas had more of their own than they could eat. Takashi Kurokawa saw his mother to the door and had turned around to leave when Mrs. Uchida insisted, "Oh stay. We are happy to have you, and you can visit with Isao and Tomomi. And Chie is here too."

Chie knew Takashi Kurokawa as one of the older boys two grades ahead of her. She was sure she had not exchanged two words with him in all the years they'd known each other. He seemed nice enough, but it would have taken a lot to convince her he was not dull. She imagined he'd probably not read a book in his life. While the older women fawned over the baby, Chie made an effort to be pleasant and hospitable, and of course Tomomi was her usual talkative and friendly self. Chie was glad Isao was there to engage with Takashi.

"You were the star of the baseball team! I bet you could have gone on to Koshien," Isao said, naming the fabled high school baseball team that was the pride of the nation.

"No. No chance. Koshien is the best of the best. We were lucky to get a tournament in the neighboring town," Takashi said, and he was not being overly modest. Their school's baseball team was mediocre at best. There was nothing outstanding about it, or their "star" hitter, now sitting with them.

"So, you're working at Kosugi Trading. How do you like it?" Takashi asked Chie.

"It's fine," she said. She didn't entertain the idea that he would address her directly, and her faint reply was hardly audible.

"I'm at Morimoto, the subcontractors. Our plant in Takaizu is just around the corner from Kosugi Trading," Takashi said.

Chie couldn't believe he might think this information would be of interest to her, and she wasn't prepared when he said, "Let's have lunch sometime."

When Chie excused herself after a decent interval, she regretted she'd let her mother press her into staying. She didn't have anything that could be called a social life in town, but she hardly thought she wanted to spend her free time with an inaka guy like Takashi Kurokawa. She may be just a country girl herself, but at least she had ideas of something more, even if they were just daydreams. She couldn't even imagine having a conversation with him. A lunch with him, alone, sounded like a nightmare. It was out of the question. Still, she found herself agreeing when he called and said he'd meet her at the local soba restaurant, a short walk from both of their offices.

"Your mother said you love soba."

Had he been investigating her? It didn't occur to Chie that her mother might have mentioned to her only friend her only daughter's favorite food.

The lunch passed amicably. When Chie said goodbye to him, she never expected to repeat the experience.

20

In the beginning, Chie thought Toshi was just being nice. After all, he'd found her a job, and then an apartment. She was grateful for the attention and interest he'd taken in her. Several times when she'd seen him in the neighborhood, she assumed he was there to attend to business related to his father's properties in the area. Running into him one evening, she was surprised he would be at the corner of her street at that time. It was a late hour for business.

"Professor Sakai. What a surprise to see you."

"Yes. My family is out this evening," he lied, "and I thought you might like to join me for dinner. I've picked up some *souzai* at the department store. They have the best prepared food."

It was eight o'clock. Chie had already eaten at the office. It had been a busy day and rather than eat late when she got home, she and the only other woman in her section had ordered out for obento, eating it at their desks.

"I've already eaten this evening," Chie said.

"I could just come up and we could share a cup of tea."

Chie thought him mildly insistent. Except for a visit from

her mother, and a fast visit from Kimiko, no one had been in her apartment.

"Well. All right." She didn't think it possible to say to her professor, who was also her benefactor, no, of course not.

After that visit, Toshi would sometimes show up at her door. He always had some pretext: "My mother's good friend in Kanzanji sends us muskmelons every season, and we have more than we can eat. Please enjoy this one," he said on one occasion and left immediately. But sometimes he'd linger, just long enough for Chie to think she might not be being polite or not showing proper gratitude. Like now when she said, "Would you like to come in?"

"I don't want to disturb you. I know you've had a full day at work."

"No. It's fine," Chie said, opening the door for him to step in. "I'll make some tea."

She would not normally drink green tea this late in the day as she found it kept her up. But she always had a lot of tea from her family, and in any case, she couldn't have offered him anything else other than a glass of water. She might have a glass of beer on the odd occasion, but she didn't keep any alcohol in her apartment. She'd taken after her mother in that the closest she came to drinking was just being with her father and Isao when they had a drink together in the evenings.

Chie was never in expectation of a visit from Professor Sakai, but she liked talking with him and it was nice to have a guest. On his last visit he'd said she should stop addressing him as sensei, that "Sakai-sensei" seemed much too formal, even unfriendly. Chie thought so, too, though of course she could not call him by his first name. Sakai-san was formal and friendly enough, though he called her by her first name, attaching the honorific, *san*.

"Professor Rosen told me about your love of literature. English literature. I'm not familiar with it, but I could introduce you to Japanese writers," Toshi said, having made a quick visual inventory of the books she had.

Chie wondered if Carl Rosen had also told him about her professing her love to him. It made her blush and uncomfortable to even think about it. And indeed, she had put this incident, this episode, to the farthest reaches of her mind. She'd meant it when she said it, but now she could feel only embarrassment. She had come to see it as a fixation with a teacher who had shown her so much regard and attention, even respect.

Now sitting with Sakai-san on the tatami, she kept her eyes on the pattern of the cushions, afraid to let her eyes meet his. She willed herself to relax, convinced Carl Rosen would never have said anything to him. She didn't know anything personal about Carl, but if she'd needed one word to describe his character, she would have said it was integrity—of the type that would not purposely expose or humiliate her.

As he'd promised, Toshi gave Chie a few Japanese novels, but she was disappointed they were all the works of men. Of course, there were many women novelists, but he didn't seem to be familiar with any of them. She wondered if he regarded them worthy of literary esteem.

"You should know the works of Mishima, Kawabata, Dazai, Tanizaki. They are the greats. All their works are masterpieces," he told her.

"Thank you, Sakai-san. I will familiarize myself with their works," Chie said, hoping he'd be pleased she would do as he instructed.

. . .

Toshi was not in regular contact with Carl these days, thinking Carl had been around long enough and adjusted to life in Takaizu, that it wasn't necessary to keep him entertained or invited to their home as often. Toshi supposed Carl had his diversions and that he was totally capable of pursuing them on his own. He was confident Carl would eventually work things out for himself, and if he didn't, there was no reason he should be Toshi's concern. He'd made a small effort to introduce Carl to a friend, an elementary school teacher who was still single. Carl showed no interest.

Toshi regularly disappeared on Saturday mornings. Yoshiko no longer asked him where he'd been, or why he was so late returning.

Spending time with Chie had now come to be a refuge for Toshi. Lately, he could hardly bear to be in his house. Yoshiko vacillated between being remote, distracted, or overly attentive, and he never knew which Yoshiko he could expect. It occurred to him more than once she might be in some mental distress, though she never said anything about how she was feeling. The children disregarded him altogether, and he felt he had no role to play in their lives now. Yoshinaga, in the full throes of adolescence, was mostly surly. Yoshiko had been strict about the children having good manners and speaking politely, but now, indulging her son to a fault, she'd answer his calls, no matter how rough, regularly bringing refreshments to his desk while he studied. Yui, just at the start of puberty, was apparently confused if she was still the little girl who wanted to be and look like her favorite manga, the yellow-haired, blue saucer–eyed "Candy Candy." At other times she'd stand in the mirror doing her best to imitate popular singing idol Momoe Yamaguchi. After she saw the movie "The Return of Ultraman" she decided the pixie-cute young star Rumi Sakakibara was the girl she most wanted to look like.

Toshi's mother nagged him constantly. In her eyes he only had shortcomings, and she accused him in no uncertain terms. He was neglectful: "Why don't you visit more often?" He'd abandoned her: "You never take me on any trips to onsen. I don't even remember the last time I was in Izu," she said, naming her favorite hot springs spot. He was remiss in not accompanying her on any of her many outings: "I missed the last sumo basho because of you. Do you think I always want to be sitting there alone? After all, I do have a son. It is not too much to expect him to accompany me on occasion." It might have been a consequence of her poor hearing that she could not modulate her voice, as she yelled into the telephone, telling him she had expected he would take her to the Takaizu Museum of Art for the recent exhibition of her favorite Nihonga artist: "Shimomura Kanzan! Who knows when I will next be able to see his work? Yesterday was the last day of the exhibition!"

To Toshi, she made it sound as though she'd never speak to him again.

"Hello. I'm sorry to bother you, Chie-san, but I thought you might like to go to the Flower Park. It's such fine weather." It was Takashi Kurokawa calling.

Most of the time Chie had no problem turning down his diffident invitations. She didn't want to be rude to a hometown neighbor, and the son of her mother's best friend. She simply wished he'd stop calling. She made an effort to be polite, agreed to have lunch with him two times, and regretted it the minute they'd sat down. She thought he was dull in the extreme and could hardly feign interest in spending any time with him. After commenting on the weather, incapable of carrying on the simplest conversation, he had nothing to say. And as she'd surmised, and he'd openly admitted, he'd never read a book in his life.

"Yes, it is fine weather today. But I'm afraid I have many tasks to attend to. Thank you for asking." Chie hoped she didn't sound horrified at his invitation.

Chie much preferred the time she spent with Sakai-san. When she was with him, she could forget about a job she knew was going nowhere and in which she'd be in the same position in one year or five. Having Toshi for company, she didn't think about the daydream future she'd planned for herself, or care that it was disappearing with each passing day. But she knew Sakai-san could not have invited her to the Flower Park, or anywhere else for that matter, however innocent the destination. They could not be seen in public. There would be no excuse for it, no way to explain it.

She now found herself being deceitful with her mother about not being able to go home every weekend. Although she had the role of the adoring aunt, she didn't feel quite as much a part of their tight little household now. Surely her presence would not be missed.

"It's unusual for the company to ask us to come in over the weekend, but there's a big negotiation coming up, and we must be prepared." She felt guilty lying to her mother.

"It is not right that they ask you to give up your weekend. And do they know your father is on his deathbed?"

"Of course not, Mother. I don't discuss personal matters at work, ever."

"They may be a company, but surely they are human. I am sure they would not ask you to come in if they knew the situation."

"Kosugi Trading is an advanced company. I am only required to work half days on Saturdays twice a month."

Chie was glad to get off the phone with her mother. She expected Sakai-san to come any minute, and if her mother had heard the doorbell ring, she would be curious who was her guest, which would require Chie to lie again, on the spot. And the very thought of her mother finding out she'd had a man in her apartment was enough to give her a headache.

Toshi's initial visits had always felt tentative, almost surreptitious. Should he really come in? Should he not? Was it all right? Now that he knew she expected him, he became comfortable and relaxed as if it were the most natural thing in the world that she would be receiving a professor and he would be visiting the home of a former student of his institution.

Although Toshi had lost the initial feeling of the inherent impropriety of the situation, he couldn't help but be aware he was putting her in a compromising position. He was drawn to her, and without his thinking about it, he found himself drifting over to her apartment as often as he could. At first he was captivated by her beauty and found enjoyment just in looking at her. This country girl with the glowing skin could have been a made-up character in the many novels he knew she read. He could hardly envision her in the place, the backwoods, he knew she was from. Toshi convinced himself his interest in her was purely whimsical. She just happened to be around, available, for company and conversation at a time his wife was not.

"My mother gets so many gifts. We can never consume it all," he said, handing her a package of expensive grapes as he walked in the door.

"Oh, these are really special," Chie said, taking the small carton in both hands. "Your mother must have a lot of friends."

"No. That's not true at all. I am sure she could count her friends on one hand. But because of my father's position, she has many people who shower her with their regard." And indeed, she was showered with obligatory *o-seibo* and *o-chūgen*, year-end and midyear gifts.

"But she must also have cultivated her own circle of friends," Chie said.

"My mother is a very self-absorbed woman. She has always been like that."

"Surely she has many good qualities as well."

"She's generous. I can say that," and Toshi knew that's all he could say because he did not want their conversation to drift into talk of his family and his mother's generosity to them.

"It is really a beautiful day. I love this time of year," Chie said, changing the subject before he could.

And this subject, too, had to be avoided, Toshi realized, as it pointed to the fact they couldn't be out enjoying the fine weather. He looked at her as she looked away, staring at nothing on the tatami.

In this moment Toshi was overwhelmed with guilt. Aside from putting this young woman in a position that may cause her to be gossiped about, he was depriving her of having a normal life. Maybe if he hadn't insinuated himself, she might be able to enjoy the company of the young man she'd mentioned, her neighbor Kurokawa-san. But he knew that man offered her nothing she was looking for. If she could be happy, satisfied, content, with a life of being a wife and mother, no doubt Kurokawa-san would be perfect. But it didn't seem to fit. There was something about her, an inner intensity that could be discerned, perhaps was most evident, in that he had never seen her laugh. Pleasant would describe her, but not happy. Toshi never was without the feeling she was not matched with the life that was hers.

21

Yoshiko gave up.

She now accepted, truly accepted for the first time, that she had chosen this life. The choice might have been a mistake, but this was her lot. She made up her mind she would not complain, not seek to get out of it. Not try to make any major changes. She still loved Toshi. But she could admit to herself she was drawn to Carl Rosen, though it was not even clear to her what it was that she found so alluring. Perhaps it was that he felt so deeply, and expressed it, and imbued with passion anything, or anyone, he cared about. For all the things she found attractive in Toshi, passion was not among them. He was a good son, despite what her mother-in-law said. He was a good father, and he'd been a good husband.

But when she was with Carl, she felt she was at the center of his world. She didn't pry, didn't ask questions, but Carl had been open about his childhood, and Yoshiko could only feel sadness that he'd been all but abandoned by his mother. Naturally he'd told her about his ex-wife, Naoko, who Yoshiko thought of as cruel. Yoshiko felt connected to Carl, as though they shared a precious secret that only they could know. She felt as though he held her heart in those hands that so attracted her. Now, she told herself it was a mistake she'd gotten so close to him, and she regretted it.

Yoshiko made up her mind to never see Carl alone again, and that was not that hard to do as there were few chances for her to be on her own. Now she decided and accepted that she would be, if not the dutiful wife, the dutiful and devoted mother. And around mothering she contrived things to do, to look for, to find, to buy, to seek out, to make—it was never-ending. Deciding Yoshinaga needed a better desk, she spent the better part of a week visiting furniture showrooms. She attended a series of afternoon classes for housewives on "The Best Nutri-tion for Young Minds" and immediately set about buying foods for dishes she prepared, not just following recipes conscien-tiously, but studying the nutritional value of every ingredient. And it wouldn't be long now before she would need to lavish similar attention on Yui. Although Yui was not the eldest child, nor the son, Yoshiko did not intend to turn her back on her daughter. She saw what happened with young girls, and that it didn't take much for them to think they were worthless simply because society didn't expect much of them. Japanese females, they were still generally raised to fit, and be content with, preset traditional roles.

Yoshiko had a few friends, but she kept her thoughts to herself. She knew Toshi was not interested in listening to her. In any case, she didn't have anything to say. She was certainly not going to confess her feelings for another man, his friend. She was not going to cry and tell him she regretted she found his friend more interesting and that she was somehow fascinated with him. She was not going to say that on some days she felt close to despair, feeling she had energy only for tears—though she never cried. Without a doubt she was depressed. But she'd never talk to anyone about it, even if there had been someone to talk to. Diminished, she even had the sense she was getting physically smaller.

Mrs. Sakai had now essentially lost her hearing, and it was exhausting to be around her. Everything had to be repeated. And in a loud voice. If she thought Yoshiko's voice was too loud, she'd angrily chastise her, saying, "Don't speak like a merchant!" When Yoshiko spoke to her in a softer voice, the older woman would say with palpable disgust that Yoshiko should "stop that infernal mumbling and speak properly." Toshi, too, was exasperated with his mother, but he managed to hide it under the guise of the dutiful son of his widowed mother.

Now Yoshiko and Toshi lived like companions. And they were hardly that, as they both contrived to pursue their individual activities on their own. She couldn't remember the last time they'd had sex—the last time they'd made love was a distant memory. They were friendly, and it was not difficult for them to be together. They were both committed to their children, their family, and would do whatever was required to keep their home stable, even if it was just for the appearance of stability.

Yoshiko not only didn't ask where Toshi went every Saturday morning, she honestly didn't care. Maybe he had found a friend, someone he could spend time and be comfortable with. She would be thankful for that. He was obviously no longer relaxed when he was at home. He'd never had a hobby, and she would be happy if he found one to occupy him, and even better if he could do it with someone. She was sorry now she had not taken up tennis when he'd suggested it years earlier. He'd said that it would be something they could do together in the coming years. She did not wish him ill, and in fact was sad and heartbroken that she no longer felt about him as she had once. But she would stay with him always. It would be a lesser life, but this was the life she chose. This is how it turned out. This is how it would be.

Yoshiko, thinking she could use a little break, took a short trip to visit her family in Matsumoto. The entire time she was there she felt she had to pretend that she, and her life, were not just fine, but good, just what she wanted. She'd never been close with her mother, but she could tell her mother knew she was not being truthful.

"And how is Mrs. Sakai?"

"She's well. Though it appears her hearing has gotten worse."

"Oh, at our age, all sorts of things go wrong, get worse. I too am *boroboro*. Falling apart."

"Oh Mother, you exaggerate. You look fine."

"*Look.*"

Her mother was the exact opposite of her mother-in-law. You'd never hear her mother complain about anything. Yoshiko knew she'd had a hard life, especially after the war, but her mother never mentioned it, never referred to it. And although her parents were sure they kept it as their own secret, Yoshiko knew her father had not just been unfaithful, but kept a mistress for years. For all she knew, he could still be keeping her. Years earlier, Yoshiko had heard her parents arguing, in hushed voices. She never forgot. Her mother, crying, had sounded like she'd choke on her muffled tears. If her mother was ashamed, or hurt, she would never have said a word—keeping a mistress was the prerogative of a man of his generation. Yoshiko had thought more than once that if he had a mistress, it was possible he also had and maintained another family. She was not going to investigate. She was willing to live with that potentiality, that mystery.

In the same way she was willing, could settle, to have a life and marriage with Toshi that was not at all what she'd hoped for. Things didn't always turn out as one hoped. She and Toshi had had some good years together. That could be enough. Whoever he had found to be a friend, it was all right with her. And in his case, she knew he would not be capable, financially or emotionally, to support an entire other family.

Although Yoshiko always preferred traveling during the day so she could get to her destination while it was still daylight, her return trip this time was an evening train, and she relished sitting on the train alone, enjoying an obento and a beer. Normally she'd have enjoyed getting lost in her favorite magazine *Kateigaho*, turning page after page of outstanding photography of places to travel, the world's best cuisine and most stylish women, and the understated luxury of Japan's most exquisite inns and hotels. But now she found contentment just looking out the window. The journey had started out bathed in sunlight, which turned into a comforting sunset. She saw house after house, some in clusters, some standing alone, all with closed curtains, and she imagined the lives of those inside. No doubt there was joy and happiness, but surely also unhappiness.

Arriving home, she didn't know whether she could expect to

find Toshi there or not, and was not surprised he wasn't. Yoshinaga was away for a school soccer tournament played out of town. Yui had gone to stay with her grandmother. The house was almost eerily quiet, which it never was between the children's coming and goings, Yui's constant chattering, and, these days, the television, frequently on, as Yoshinaga had to see every soccer game.

Yoshiko stayed up after her bath, thinking Toshi would walk in any minute. She turned on the television and mindlessly watched the screen in front of her. She fell asleep on the sofa, and now it was past midnight. She left the downstairs lights on for Toshi, thinking that even if he came in later, at least the house would not be completely dark and unwelcoming.

Forgetting to close the curtains, which Toshi always did, she woke up with the sun in her eyes. It was still early, and she could hear the door close as Toshi came in. She heard him come upstairs and wash up.

He entered their bedroom saying, "Good morning."

22

Toshi sleeping with Chie was the natural progression of the relationship developing between them. But he could not pretend it was a love affair.

"I feel guilty I've stolen your virginity," Toshi told her.

"I'm not a young girl from whom things can be taken without my permission," Chie said, blushing red with embarrassment, and some anger too.

"You should be with a man your own age. Someone with whom you have the possibility of a future, a life," Toshi said with all earnestness. No matter how he tried to deny or close his eyes to it, there was never a time he was not thinking this relationship could only have a dead-end. It could go nowhere. He couldn't even dignify their being together by calling it an affair, something two adults could throw themselves into wholeheartedly, even if guiltily. His facial expressions displayed a thin but unmistakable shield of guilt, and the same shield covered his heart. It was not just about how he felt he'd ruined Chie and her chances, but cheating on Yoshiko also meant he was not the father he meant to be to his children. *The best thing a man can do for his children is love and honor their mother.* He'd heard that somewhere and couldn't forget it. He might have been able to carry on an affair with Chie if he'd been happy, but wracked with self-reproach and a conscience that would not let him forget he was bringing shame on so many people, principally himself, left him deeply miserable.

"Our being together may not be what I'd imagined my first love would be. I know you don't love me. That's all right. You have shown me a glimpse of love, and I am happy with that," Chie told him.

"You deserve more. At the least, I'd like to take you out," Toshi said as he dressed to leave.

"That's not necessary," Chie said. "I am happy just to be with you."

"One day maybe we can take a trip," Toshi said, though knowing as he said it that it would not be possible. If he were to ever be discovered having an affair, and with a former student from the college, he'd lose his position immediately. The last thing he would ever do is jeopardize his ability to support his family. His great contradiction was that he wanted to flirt with the idea, the role, of being a rebel, someone outside of society and societal norms, while knowing in his deepest heart he never was, never could be, that rebel. He was conventional in all things, wanted to follow the rules, stick to what was accepted, the traditional ways. Marrying Yoshiko was probably the wildest thing he'd ever done. But now, he saw she was slipping into a traditional role. He lamented it. Because what had held them together, what he found attractive, is that she was so different from him. She was willing to take risks, lead, not follow. She'd always been her own woman. It gave their marriage balance, precisely because she was not like him. But these days he saw her as the typical housewife, uninteresting, even boring. He wasn't sure of the cause and didn't take responsibility for it. It occurred to him she might be at the "change of life" but knew she was definitely too young to be going through menopause.

"Toshi, when will you come again?" Chie was now comfortable calling him by his first name.

"Next Saturday. Maybe. I can't say for sure."

A simple question to which he could not give a simple answer. Everything he did depended on his work, his family. He was not available.

They lingered at the door, embracing. Chie wished he'd never leave. She loved the warm feeling of his body next to hers. The smell of him was now familiar and comforting. She kissed his neck, below the ear, her favorite spot on his body. Without either of them meaning for it to happen, he was now aroused. Within seconds, both fully dressed, they were making love on the tatami mat.

Mr. Uchida died.

What had been expected, happened. There was no one on Uchida Road who didn't know Hiroshi Uchida would soon be given his *kaimyo*, Buddhist name after death. The funeral arrangements were just as he had planned, an extended affair of the *otsuya*, wake, with all the neighbors in attendance. The *osoushiki* was the full Buddhist funeral ritual. In attendance were relatives Chie didn't know they had, as they sat for what seemed like hours while the priest intoned long incantations. Much of it was incomprehensible, but it was clear all the ringing of bells, the ceremonial robes, tassels, and other regalia could only be about death. It was an expensive affair, and Chie was sorry her mother was spending money she could surely better use otherwise. But she knew, too, this expense had been planned for, and her parents had saved. Her father, the man who couldn't stand any of the customary social rituals while he was alive, wanted an elaborate send-off. He hadn't been as enthusiastically engaged in anything in the years leading to this death as he'd been with *soushiki no shuukatsu*, funeral planning, and at the end he didn't do anything else. Before entering the hospital for the last time, from first thing in the morning until he fell asleep, where he sat at the small central table, he put all the energy he had left into putting the finishing touches on his funeral.

Chie's mother, who had not had a sick day in her life, would be dead two years to the day later.

Isao, now head of the household, was conscientious in assuming this role. All memory of him riding a bicycle to and from school and spending his days playing catch with boyhood friends were now forgotten. Tomomi, pregnant with their second child, had settled in so firmly, it appeared she'd always lived on Uchida Road. She knew how to keep up contacts, who to visit when sick, who to give the seasonal gifts. She wrote by hand the stack of *nengajo*, the New Year's greeting cards, they would persist in sending.

For her part, Chie had stopped making excuses not to go home. She just didn't go. She wasn't missed.

Mainly she avoided meeting up with people, and though the last person she wanted to see or spend time with was Kimiko, she showed up at Chie's door, fashionably dressed and made up, though she was going nowhere. Chie knew she couldn't keep dodging Kimiko but wished she would at least telephone. But of course that would have been the polite thing to do, not what

Kimiko would do. Chie dreaded the possibility of Toshi being there when Kimiko made one of her unannounced visits.

"Sure, you work full time, but don't tell me you never have time to go out and have fun. What do you do all the time? I know you're not going home. My mother told me no one even remembers the last time you were in Yano village or on Uchida Road."

"I do go there. I was there just a few days ago. I went straight from work."

"But you're never there on the weekends. Especially on Saturdays. I know because I've been there, and I've also tried to get in touch. It's like you're trying to disappear. Or hide."

"Oh, Kimiko. You're always so dramatic. I don't 'disappear,' and I am not hiding. I have a job. And when I'm not working, I just prefer to stay at home, reading, by myself."

"By yourself?"

"Yes. It may seem odd to you, but I really prefer to be alone."

"I don't think it's odd because I know you've always been like that. I had to practically drag you kicking and screaming to my wedding."

"Kimi, you know that's not true!"

"Do I?"

Chie was now just tired of this contentious relationship she had with Kimiko and felt it had always been that way. They were in no way compatible but had just been 'best friends' as a matter of course, and reality. There were no other girls their age on Uchida Road, and Kimiko never had a friend at school.

"When are you going to get a boyfriend, Chie Uchida? You know you can't wait around forever."

"I'm not waiting around. I am just not in a hurry. Besides, I haven't found the person I want to be with, to marry."

"My mother tells me Takashi Kurokawa's mother says he would give anything to be with you, but all you do is rebuff him."

"I've gone out with him several times. I just don't see it going any further than that. We are not suited for one another. I find him impossibly dull."

"He's not like that teacher you were so crazy about—what's his name? The American professor. But I think you had better start being realistic. You know what they say about 'Christmas cake.'"

Chie refused to respond to this. Yes, she knew Christmas cake referred to young women who were past a desirable age to marry. She thought it was a stupid saying, and cruel, and she certainly was not applying the saying to herself. She wanted to tell Kimiko she was wrong: Chie was with a man who found her desirable, and she was in no hurry to marry someone just because it was supposed to be time to do it. But the last person on this earth Chie would have confided in was Kimiko, her best friend.

When Carl dropped by Toshi's office, he made no mention of the fact that Toshi had said he'd call him, or come by, never did, and never offered any excuses. He couldn't say that Toshi had become distant, only that they were not as close as they'd been. But as there was no animosity between them, he intended to just ignore it. And besides, he knew Toshi had obligations of family that did not give him the freedom and time that Carl had.

"It's been a while. How are you doing? How's the family?" Carl asked Toshi.

"Couldn't be better. And yeah, we really haven't seen much of each other lately."

"I've been hoping to catch up with you," Carl said

Frankly, he was eager to talk with Toshi. These days Carl's thoughts were mainly centered on his future. He didn't have any plans, but he was no longer content to coast along, as he always had. He'd always let things just happen, but now felt the door on that kind of life was closing. A colleague as well as a friend, Toshi was the best person Carl could confide in.

"I'm sorry about missing our last date. Something came up, and honestly, I just forgot all about it. When I telephoned, you were out," Toshi said.

"Oh, no problem," Carl assured him.

Carl was probably the first person in Takaizu to have an answering machine installed. It had seemed like a ridiculous thing, totally unnecessary, and even though he was home a lot, he hated the idea of missing a call. Maybe it would be Yoshiko. He had no idea why Toshi would bother to say he had called, why he felt it necessary to lie. It wasn't like Toshi to do so, but then, Carl wasn't sure *what* was like Toshi. Carl always felt Toshi had a side that he kept to himself, and Carl imagined it would be easy for Toshi to have secrets. Sure, he had invited Carl into his family life for various occasions, but Toshi's true personal life, his inner life, was off limits. There were just things he didn't talk about because he never talked about his private life, never revealed anything of himself, his feelings. It was one of the reasons Carl thought Yoshiko and Toshi were poorly matched.

"What about having dinner with me on Saturday? Just the

two of us," Carl said. "It's really been a long time. Nothing fancy. You come to my apartment. I'll pick up some gyoza. We could have a few beers."

"Oh, Saturday is no good," Toshi said.

Toshi spent every Saturday with Chie. He'd usually go to her place in the afternoon and stay until evening. He was no longer even expected to be at home Saturday evenings.

"I see."

"*Chotto,*" Toshi said.

And Carl knew from that one word, he should not inquire further.

"I *will* call," Toshi said. He was seemingly unaware that lingering on "will" made it clear he hadn't called before. "I'll find the time, and we can get together like old times."

23

Things were unraveling.

Toshi's world was now one in which his only emotion was guilt, and that feeling blocked out all other feeling. Although he was usually congenial, these days it was unusual to see a smile on his face. At the college, he moved along the corridors ghostlike, neglecting to exchange a glance or even customary greeting with colleagues. With all the welcome promise of spring, normally at this time of year he would have had some sense of satisfaction at releasing another graduation class into the world like so many doves of peace.

This Saturday, instead of going directly to Chie's apartment he wandered into a ramen shop and gobbled up a bowl of hot ramen at the counter. Toshi lost time as he sat, entranced, watching the chef prepare bowl after bowl with machine-like efficiency, and took no notice of the lunchtime line of customers waiting for a seat.

When he showed up at Chie's he was annoyed to find she had prepared a meal.

"Chie, you really shouldn't bother with these meals. You are just wasting money." He frowned like he was admonishing a child.

"I don't spend a lot. Besides, it's nice to make something nice for you, for us."

He knew she was trying to give their relationship a sense of normalcy, making it appear his spending time with her was ordinary. But there was nothing ordinary or casual about this relationship for Toshi. No longer so relaxed when he visited, he was wary, his eyes shifting like he was looking over his shoulder even though they were alone. Now his eyes fell on the small dresser drawer in the corner of the room. Chie had emptied one of the drawers so he could leave some clothes there, but he steadfastly refused. Aware evidence could be discovered, he was more than a little cautious about not leaving a trail.

They sat at the table without talking. Toshi stared at the small wall clock with its orange plastic frame, green hands, and red numbers. Assailed by its garishness, he was reminded this country girl had no taste and lacked aesthetic sense whether it be in furnishings or clothes. It seemed she would wear anything. He couldn't help but compare her with Yoshiko, who dressed in effortless style and would rather not know the time than to put something so ugly on the wall. Anyhow, he didn't want to be reminded of the time because he knew whatever time it was, he should be home.

He had planned to spend the day with Chie but was ready to go after spending less than an hour at the apartment.

"I've got some errands to take care of today," Toshi said, and got up from the table. He thought for a moment to embellish this story saying he needed to take his son to cram school but caught himself since he'd already told Chie his wife, whose name he never mentioned, took care of everything for the kids.

"Of course," Chie said, adding, "though I'd hoped you would stay longer."

"Not today. I can't," Toshi said, already at the door.

"I'm glad you came, even for a short time," Chie said.

She stayed sitting at the table. If she'd looked in a mirror, she would have seen the understanding smile she'd given Toshi when he left still on her face, plastered there like a mask. She looked at the table set for two with *hashioki*, the chopstick rests she'd just bought, coasters, a small vase of flowers. The tableau, like her smile, was part of a charade. She wouldn't let herself think about Toshi's family. She had not even conjured an image of his wife. Chie was not curious about who his wife could be, or what she looked like. She was expert in not allowing herself to think about or imagine Toshi's life when he was not with her. All that mattered to Chie was her belief that she was genuinely sharing a life with someone she loved. And although she knew he could not love her fully, she was willing to accept the affection he could give her.

The worst part for her was hiding their relationship. There was no time she didn't feel the strain of it. The machinations, the dishonesty and outright lying were wearing on her. She wanted the love, the attention he showered on her when they were together—she just wished it could have been simpler, open, and shared. She wanted everyone to know what she'd found, what she and Toshi had between them. Preparing little attractive meals was how she worked at pretending they had, not just a life, but a home life together. Sharing a meal normalized their trysts: he wasn't just dropping by. They had a home together, and it didn't matter if he didn't want to leave clothes there.

She may have been a dreamer, but she'd put all romantic notions out of her head and convinced herself being with Toshi was worth missing a conventional relationship with dates and the occasional outing. And if she really wanted to go out, there was always Takashi Kurokawa, who continued to contact her on the slimmest of excuses. Either he was truly obtuse or he just did not take offense at his invitations regularly being turned down.

Yoshiko was now sleepwalking through her marriage, through life. She knew, she was certain, Toshi was having an affair. He was cheating, but what upset her most was his not being open, not being honest. It made her angry that he didn't tell her, that he didn't own up to acting on his desires. It diminished him in her eyes because he tried to cover it up like a child. Did he think she was stupid? Blind? Respect meant more to her than trust, and he had lost her respect. Yoshiko could admit to herself she was curious about who the woman was, who she could be, but she didn't really care. After all, if one's husband is finding love and having sex with another woman, how much is necessary to know about that person? But she cared enough to think that the other woman, too, was being treated unfairly. She thought this unknown woman must suffer from being with a man who was not truly available to her.

Yoshiko couldn't say what it was that made her pick up the telephone and call Carl Rosen that afternoon. It appeared entirely spontaneous, but she'd been planning to do it for some time. Today seemed perfect: she was alone, again.

"Yoshiko, how nice to hear from you. Hear your voice."

It had been months since they'd talked.

"We haven't seen you for a long time," she said, and immediately corrected herself. "I haven't seen you. I just thought I'd say hello." She dropped the pretense. "Actually, I thought we might meet. For a coffee or something." She'd already ruled out the idea of meeting in the evening and drinking wine.

"Sure, Yoshiko. Anytime."

"What about today? I'm free. And Toshi's not around."

"Don't I remember your Saturdays were always spent with Mrs. Sakai, at her house?"

"Not these days. Yoshinaga and Yui are busy with their activities, school clubs, and this and that. My mother-in-law has been in poor health and seems to prefer we do not go there. And Toshi is always occupied on Saturdays now."

They met at a coffee shop in Carl's neighborhood. Both so anxious to talk, so happy to catch up, so obviously missing each other's company that they never took one sip of the expertly brewed coffee.

"He won't like it if we don't drink the the coffee. And eat his poundcake. He makes it himself," Carl told Yoshiko, casting his eyes at the coffee shop owner, who sat on a tall stool behind the counter.

The owner came over and took away the cups of now-cold coffee, saying, "I'll bring you fresh cups," and mumbled, "Eat the cake. It's good."

"Yes, it is!" Carl said bowing his head to the owner. "I always enjoy it."

"So, you come here often?" Yoshiko said.

"Yes, this is one of my favorite places in the neighborhood. I like that he clearly takes pride in his coffee, and his cake. And it's kind of cozy since it's dark in here day or night."

"And I'm sure he likes having such an appreciative customer. You see, you are loyal."

"I guess I am," Carl said. "I'd especially like to be thought of as a loyal friend to you."

"I've always thought of you as a loyal friend."

"And your loyal friend is happy to tell you that you look really well."

"Well, I am managing," Yoshiko said.

She always managed to look good, no matter what her physical condition or emotional state. Her countenance and figure always combined to make her look like someone one wanted to compliment. "Managing?"

Yoshiko didn't reply.

"I've been wanting to talk with Toshi, but we can't seem to arrange to get together," Carl said.

"He can be difficult to pin down these days," Yoshiko said.

"Yoshiko, I'm thinking about leaving Takaizu. I don't really have a plan. It's just an idea, and I haven't worked out the details."

"I see," Yoshiko said, her voice dropping a little. "But Carl, you need to have a plan."

"I have a few possibilities. If I leave Japan I might be able to get a position at the college in Boston where I taught for a short time. I have some friends and colleagues there, so in a way it would be a ready-made community."

"Truthfully, Carl, I can't see you making a life here. Of course, you can make a place for yourself in Japanese society, in general, but I don't think this place has anything to offer you, really. Takaizu has it charms, but it's much too provincial. I see you thriving in a place that's more cosmopolitan."

"I guess more 'cosmopolitan' could mean a place where I might find a woman to be with," Carl said.

"Yes, it could mean that."

"I haven't lost hope," Carl said.

"Carl. I know we haven't seen each other for months, but knowing you are near has been a comfort. I will not hesitate to tell you that the potential loss of your friendship is an unbearable thought for me."

"For me as well," Carl said, his voice cracking. "But I think it's time. I've been in Takaizu three years now, which I think is long enough to know if it worked or not."

"I understand."

"I plan to talk with Toshi. He's always clearheaded. I'd like to know what he thinks."

"Toshi is having an affair."

Yoshiko said this coolly, but it hit Carl like someone threw a rock in his face.

"What?"

"He's having an affair. I cannot say with whom because I do not know."

"Oh, Yoshiko, I'm so sorry. I don't know what to say."

"You needn't say anything, Carl. I am not particularly upset by it. I just dislike his dishonesty. And neglect of me, as a person, even if not as a wife."

Later that night when Carl was alone, he reflected that his getting so close with Yoshiko was something to be regretted. When he thought how close, dangerously close, they'd come to having an affair, he felt a chill. Neither he nor Yoshiko would have been satisfied with a secret affair. To do it would mean to lose all integrity. Just thinking of it, he was reminded of the many scoundrels his mother had brought into his life. He hated them all, disliking intensely that they took advantage of his mother, didn't care about her at all. He knew Yoshiko would not have denied the possibility of having an affair, and she would never hide it. It would have to be open, whether she and Toshi had agreed to an open marriage or not. Honesty would have to prevail, regardless of who knew, who might be hurt.

It was early evening when Yoshiko got home. She was surprised to see Toshi had already come back.

"I didn't know you would be here for dinner. I'll put something together."

"You don't have to bother," Toshi said, moving to the refrigerator. "I can just heat up some leftovers."

"I'll cook," Yoshiko said, placing the cutting board on the counter.

In no time, she'd put together a *do-nabe* to be cooked and eaten at the table. This one-pot dish, while not festive, was usually a communal meal served when the whole family was together.

"I saw Carl today. We had coffee together."

"Oh?"

"Yes. We haven't seen him in a while, haven't invited him. I just thought I'd see how he's doing."

"And how is he doing? He told me he wants to get together. Just me and him."

"Yes, he mentioned that. And said you didn't seem to have time."

"I'll make time. It's just the end of the year—there's always a lot to do around putting in last grades, graduation."

Yoshiko didn't bother to reply or comment. It seemed unnecessary. And she didn't want to listen to his lies and excuses. They had nothing to say to one another. She didn't need to converse and disliked conversation that had, as its purpose, the avoidance of silence. What a contrast, she couldn't help thinking, as she and Carl could talk nonstop. Yoshiko and Toshi were practically like strangers now.

It had all fallen apart so fast, Toshi thought to himself. It all—family, his job, the new house—seemed so meaningless now. He could only wonder that this, this emptiness he felt at the core of his being, was what he had strived for all his life. He remembered his father saying toward the end of his life that all a man has is his family. No matter how much he works, builds a career, earns, and puts away money, "at the end there is only family." That was odd coming from his father, Toshi thought, and he wondered if his father was repeating something he'd heard. Mr. Sakai was fond of aphorisms and sayings and seemed to have one for every occasion. He had never particularly cared about family. He was there, he was around, but he was never engaged and barely interacted with his wife and son. In a vow he'd never openly stated, Toshi told himself he would not be that kind of man, father, or husband. But here he was, his father's son. *Ringo ga ki kara tōku ni ochiru koto wa arimasen.* "Apples never fall far from the tree," his father occasionally said. That couldn't always be true, Toshi thought. He had no plan to be like his father, whose life he saw as a series of acquiring things: golf clubs, good whiskey, property. Marrying the "correct" woman, having a *chounan*, son and heir, Mr. Sakai had followed a script, one that had been written for him long before he was born. Even as he followed convention, Toshi's plan had been to fall far and roll away.

When Toshi didn't show up the following week, Chie had more than foreboding—she knew it was the end.

She stood staring out her window, the curtains drawn back just enough so she could see the beautiful day she was missing. The bus that went to the Flower Park stopped in the street opposite her building. She thought if she just went downstairs and caught the bus it was possible she could still catch the last of the cherry blossoms. She loved this season and accepted denying herself this pleasure. She stayed in, thinking that if Toshi came she would want to be there. She had tried to give him a key, but he refused to take it. If he telephoned and she were out, she'd miss his call and have no way of knowing whether he'd called or not. She couldn't call him. Even if she'd wanted to take that chance, she didn't have his telephone number. He wouldn't have given it to her even if she'd asked, and she'd never ask. If he were to show up, she couldn't even ask him why he hadn't come earlier, or before. She had no rights, and she knew it.

As the afternoon passed and darkness fell on the tiny apartment, she saw her life in all its sparse reality. Shadows fell on the room, seeming to outline all her life's deficiencies. She could not get over this feeling of always wanting something, undefined, but always out of reach. The darkening shadows emphasized the tawdriness of the cheap table and chairs, sofa, and lamps with which she'd furnished her apartment. Her attempts to brighten the place with a few plants and occasional fresh flowers now all seemed artificial. None of her dreams came true. But she refused to give herself up to this despair she felt in a place right below her heart. Maybe it had been a mistake to get into this relationship with Toshi, but she didn't feel she'd done anything wrong. She deserved to be happy, to have a man be kind to her. She deserved to be loved. A professor, intelligent and sensitive . . . She could talk to him, and she knew he enjoyed talking with her. But it was clear their being together was always enveloped in a gossamer-thin veil of make-believe. This wasn't real, and never could be. Yes, this first relationship was precious, but she knew she could not truly be loved by someone who was not available.

From that day, three weeks would go by before she heard from Toshi. He didn't come to her apartment. He didn't telephone. He sent her a letter.

Dear Chie,

I hope this brief letter will find you well. The weather has been fine, and I hope you have been enjoying it. The cherry blossoms seem to be lingering longer than usual this year.

I knew this day would come, but it has come sooner than I thought. I will not see you anymore. I have been wrong to start a relationship with you and I must end it, now. I was wrong to take your time, was wrong to let you give yourself to me. And of course, I was wrong to be unfaithful to my wife. All in all, I have been a dishonorable man, and I regret it entirely.

You are a smart young woman and a good person. I hope you will have a good life, and I am sure you will.

Sincerely,
Toshinaga Sakai

And with that, the relationship was ended. Chie was not shocked, or even surprised. She felt it coming but had made up stories in her head with a different ending. She had no way to prepare for this, and the best she could do was try to pretend otherwise. But she could tell during his last visits, and even more during their lovemaking, that he was not truly with her. More than just preoccupied, he was unhappy. She knew he felt guilty, and indeed, he'd told her so many times—too many times for her to believe him when he'd told her, in the same breath, that he loved her.

This had been an interlude, in both of their lives. Toshi had a family to return to.

Chie had nothing.

24

"Thanks so much for inviting me," Carl said. "It's really kind of you." Handing Toshi the bottle of champagne he had brought, he said, "I think it's a good one. At the least, we can enjoy a last toast together."

"You really didn't need to bring anything," Toshi said. "This is our dinner for you. Yoshiko has been cooking for days. And my mother has made her famous pot-au-feu. She's especially good at preparing *furansu ryori*. But we decided to have *washoku*, Japanese cuisine, too. Why not? After all, it's a farewell party, so let's indulge. Come in, come in, sit."

It didn't seem like all that long ago they had all sat at this long, low table when Carl first arrived in Takaizu. Carl reflected that exactly three years had passed since he first stepped into their home, first met Yoshiko. Now entering the room, she seemed to glide, and he was reminded of what he felt when he first laid eyes on her—rare, beautiful, exquisite.

"Carl, so good of you to come. We're all so glad to see you," Yoshiko said.

The table was laid out from end to end with a feast, and he

couldn't imagine where there would be room to place the platter Yoshiko now brought in.

Carl uttered all the normal politenesses: *Oh, you shouldn't have. You went to all this trouble for me, I apologize for the imposition. It is too kind.*

They responded with the customary replies: *Oh it's nothing. We hardly have anything. We hope we can satisfy your palate with this simple meal that we just whipped up.*

Truly appreciative, Carl complimented everyone and everything, and was particularly attentive to the ceramic ware.

"I love Arita-yaki," he said, picking up a small dish for shoyu, soy sauce.

"Yes, I remember you said so. That first time you made dinner for us at your apartment. I love it too! It's my favorite." Yoshiko was more animated than usual. "It is fine, but yet not delicate."

"You two are so particular about dishes, but I prefer the *Mashiko-yaki.* It's attractive and solid. I'm never worried about breaking it," Toshi said. "But Yoshiko would never let us use that ceramic ware for a special dinner."

Mrs. Sakai came in, bowing slowly, and took the place at the head of the table.

"It is so nice to see you again, Mrs. Sakai."

"And you as well, Mr. Rosen."

"I trust you are in good health."

With that, Mrs. Sakai was given liberty to give Carl an account of her ailments.

"I'm afraid my health is not good. But I have many acquaintances who are in worse health so I cannot complain. But worst of all I've had to submit to wearing hearing aids. I do not really need them, but young people these days are always mumbling."

Carl could hardly respond with more than a polite "I see."

"I am told you are returning to your home in the United States of America."

"Yes. Massachusetts. It's not really my home, but I used to live there."

"Then just where is your *furusato*, Mr. Rosen?"

"Oh, Mother," Toshi chimed in, "not everyone is so concerned with having a traditional hometown to return to. Carl is a modern man."

"I'm sure he is," Mrs. Sakai said.

During the meal, Yoshiko was at her most engaging. Conversation came easy, and she was as comfortable talking with Carl as if they'd been alone. And she was keenly aware they would never be alone again.

"Carl, we haven't known you to have a small appetite. Please have some more of Mrs. Sakai's dish. It really is special. She has studied French cooking."

Yoshiko now took every opportunity to praise or say something nice about her mother-in-law. She'd vowed to herself she would do everything necessary to remove any tension between her and the older woman. She earnestly hoped to never again raise her mother-in-law's suspicions.

"Oh, Yoshiko. I hardly 'studied.' I took a few lessons. But I can say I was one of the more adept students."

"Mother, your famed modesty is showing, in praise of your own 'famous' dish," Toshi said.

"It's delicious. I don't want to eat up everything," Carl said, accepting another plate of food from Yoshiko.

"That's not possible with Yoshinaga and Yui around,"

Yoshiko said in response. The children, no longer little kids, came in, gobbled up inordinate amounts, and were soon gone back to their rooms.

"What a feast this is," Carl said, helping himself to the myriad dishes on the table.

"You must definitely try this octopus." Yoshiko held out a small dish with two hands. "It's marinated for two days with pickled plum."

Thoroughly enjoying himself, in this moment Carl wondered why he was leaving. He had these good friends, and their warm home where he was welcome. Yes, Toshi had been distant for a time, but he had redoubled his efforts and made time to spend with Carl in the last weeks. When Carl discussed his plans about leaving, Toshi seemed truly sorry to hear it and told Carl how much he'd miss him. He said he was especially glad Carl thought enough of him and their friendship to confide in him and seek his guidance.

"It's great having this chance to host you. I know I haven't really been available these past months," Toshi said, his voice trailing. "Just so much going on."

"Oh, no problem," Carl said. "I know you have your work and obligations."

"Takaizu can be a dreary place without connections and things to do," Toshi said.

"I found things to do. It hasn't been bad at all. And Yoshiko has been diligent in telling me about all the entertainment to be enjoyed here." Carl turned his glance toward Yoshiko. "She's been more than generous with her time in keeping me company."

"I've enjoyed it too," Yoshiko said. "It's been years since I went out to hear music."

"I'm genuinely glad you two hit it off and enjoyed so many of the same things. I'm grateful to her for stepping up and being the friend I wasn't," Toshi said, looking abashed.

"Nonsense. I've valued your friendship," Carl said. And to Yoshiko: "You have truly been kind. Thank you for everything."

"It's been my pleasure," Yoshiko said, and a smile appeared on her perfect lips.

It was past nine o'clock when Mrs. Sakai daintily wiped her mouth with a small napkin she discreetly took from the *futokoro* of her kimono and made her apologies to leave.

"We are happy, indeed honored, to have you spend your last evening in Takaizu with us. Toshinaga will miss you greatly. As I am sure Yoshiko will too," Mrs. Sakai said, nodding slightly in Yoshiko's direction.

"I am the one honored to have been invited. It has been a pleasure meeting you, Mrs. Sakai."

"Now, if you will excuse me, I will take my leave. We old people must retire at an early hour." Mrs. Sakai bowed deeply, her head almost touching the tatami.

"I am grateful for your kind consideration and generous hospitality," Carl said, bowing deeply in return.

Yoshiko began clearing away the dishes, telling Toshi not to help but to keep Carl company.

"He'll think I'm *teishukanpaku*, one of those old-fashioned husbands who never help and expect everything to be done for them."

"No, he won't. He knows you." Yoshiko left the room with a tray full of dishes.

"Let's stretch our legs and hang out on the sofa," Toshi said. "I can only sit at these low tables for so long. My mother, and Yoshiko too, can sit seiza for hours."

Going into the living room, Carl remarked with appreciation that they had in the same minute been in a traditional Japanese room like the one they'd just dined in, and now were in an entirely different one. The experience was not unlike getting on an airplane in one country and getting off in a different one. In this room, which Toshi told him Yoshiko designed and furnished, it was all simple Scandinavian. Neutral colors dominated and stood in stark contrast to many so-called "Western" rooms he'd seen. Carl remembered the living room at Mrs. Sakai's house with its heavy dark furniture, ornate brocade upholstery, a chandelier, and, everywhere, knickknacks and souvenirs from every time she went to a sumo tournament out of town.

"What about some cognac? I have an excellent bottle my father used to drink. We've hardly touched it."

Just as Toshi was about to serve it in whiskey glasses, Yoshiko came in and put Finnish glassware in front of them.

"It's better to drink it in these," she said, and the beautifully designed glasses really did seem to enhance the taste, making it not just a drink but an experience.

Carl had also brought as a parting gift a Bill Evans album. "You know I'm not crazy about this stuff, but I'll play it, in honor of you," Toshi said, putting on the record. The large fluorescent light in the *washitsu*, Japanese-style room, where they had dinner was the only flaw in that room. Now, with low incandescent lighting, the jazz piano, and drinks, it all came together to replicate those intoxicating evenings Carl and Yoshiko had spent together.

"How are you getting to the airport?" Toshi asked, bringing him back to the present.

"Oh, I've arranged everything. And thanks again for helping me get rid of my furniture." Carl had parted with his furniture as easily as he'd acquired it. But he was having every book shipped back.

"I'd wanted to give some books to that student, Chie Uchida, but I didn't know how to get in touch with her."

"I wouldn't know either," Toshi said.

"Didn't you help her find a job?"

"I did. But she's now quit."

"She was really a bright girl. I'm sure it would've been hard for her to be satisfied with an office job."

"She went back to her village. She got married. To a local guy. I told you that's how it would go."

"Toshi, it isn't always so clear how things will turn out. You seemed to think this young woman's fate was a settled matter. Maybe she had other plans for herself." Yoshiko had been quiet, as if in a reverie while she listened to the jazz, but now entered their exchange freely.

"Yes, that may be true. But the opportunities for these young women are limited."

"Maybe it's the situations that they are put in that is limiting," Yoshiko said.

"Things are changing in Japan," Toshi said, looking at Carl, "but not so fast. Maybe at another time, in the future, things could turn out differently. But I look at things as practically as I can. I am no romantic."

"It is not necessary to be a 'romantic,' as you say, to have hopes for a young woman to have a fully realized life," Yoshiko said.

"Maybe her life is fully realized now that she is married. That's how they all end up."

"Yes, Toshi, maybe it is. But maybe not. I do not know this person, have never laid eyes on her. But I must say I dislike that this former student is being so summarily disregarded."

"I don't think we need to dwell on the circumstances of this young woman," Toshi said. "No doubt things have worked out just fine."

"Well, I hope for the best for her. I was fond of her," Carl said. "And I suppose it is like you say, Toshi, she now has a good life back in her hometown."

"I'm sure that's the case," Toshi said.

Carl stood up.

His body felt heavy, almost weighted down with the intensity of the sentiment that overwhelmed him in the moment.

"This experience of living and working here would not have been the same without you both. Without your friendship. Things didn't turn out as I'd hoped, and yes, I did hope that I might settle here, might meet someone and have a family."

"It may yet happen, Carl. Don't give up," Toshi said.

"I wish you all the best," Yoshiko said. She didn't cry but her eyes were glassy.

For that moment the three of them dropped the formalities and Carl embraced Toshi and Yoshiko in turn.

And with that, he was gone from their lives.

25

It was like she'd never left.

It had been two years now since Chie returned to Yano. She'd thought when she left to go to college that she would never again live in the little village below a mountain and beside a river that was always too cold. There had never been anything for her there, there was never supposed to be. It was simple, if she just followed in the footsteps of those before her. She would be, if not happy, content. It was a plain, and good enough, life.

Her mother lived long enough to see her married to her dear friend's son, and nothing could have made her happier. Again, it was simple. Takashi Kurokawa was there and available. It was as if it had been ordained. Her mother always thought, and told Chie, that one could search far and wide, but the best things are always close to home. Apart from welcoming a third grandchild from Isao and Tomomi, Chie returning to their village was all her mother could wish for. Still, Chie knew her mother lamented that she would now work in the fields. Chie helped her mother get over this concern and disappointment by assuring her that her dear friend, Mrs. Kurokawa, would be kind, welcoming, and not work her too hard. But she saw her mother was pained, in her last year, seemingly unable to accept her lovely, lily-like daughter donning the clothes of a farm woman, tending and picking tea, pruning mikan trees, and, in season, constantly planting daikon radishes.

When Chie returned home, at first it was just a place to be after she quit her job and gave up her apartment. Isao and Tomomi welcomed her, and they were happy to have an additional hand to help with the house, farm work, and children.

Takashi Kurokawa hadn't followed her back to the village, but he did show up around the same time she returned. "My mother can no longer handle the chores on her own," he'd said. And he'd said that in the sentence following the one in which he'd asked her to marry him. Chie agreed, feeling she no longer had a good reason to resist. And she felt she could give her ailing mother this one last bit of solace.

The wedding was a simple affair with just their families present. Kimiko, having heard from her own mother that they were getting married, invited herself, saying, "I invited you," and repeating, "even if you had to be dragged kicking and screaming." She added, "Anyway, Takashi is a good guy. I once had my eye on him when we were at school. You'll soon have a gaggle of kids, and all will be bliss. You'll see. You will love married life. Even if I don't."

Chie paid no attention to all this. She wasn't looking for or expecting happiness now, not even satisfaction. She felt she was settling into the life that was already planned for her, from the beginning, whether she accepted it or not. And she had been denying it all her life. Now, all her dreams and reading and schooling seemed like such a long time ago, and that they had had nothing to do with her, really. Where had it gotten her? Into a job she didn't want. And a relationship that started in deceit and carried on with the certain knowledge it would end.

No one would have thought the sun would come out.

It had rained all through the night, falling in heavy drops on the roof and slapping the windows. Chie lay awake in her futon, unsettled by the incessant downpour. It was still raining in the early morning, the sky and clouds a uniform gray. Now, just past dawn, the sun shone brightly through white, happy clouds. All was green, pink, and blue. And quiet.

During the night, any small sound made her uneasy. She'd lie awake, thought touching memory, until her mind, exhausted with itself, fell into a fitful sleep again. Although she wasn't expected to start preparing breakfast until five thirty, she usually awoke at four. This hour and a half were both welcome solitude and sanctuary.

"Chie, wake up. We need to get started." Her mother-in-law rapped with a solid fist on the wall, not the sliding door.

"Yes, Mother. I'll be right there." Chie noiselessly slipped out of her futon. Takashi, still asleep, had not stirred at the loud rapping. When he woke, when he was ready, he would do so in one movement. He never lingered but went from deep sleep to standing on his feet in seconds. Even after two years of marriage it surprised her.

Letting her *nemaki*, cotton sleeping robe, fall around her, she was dressed in a minute.

"What a lazy girl you are," her mother-in-law said as Chie stepped into the kitchen. "If you're awake, why don't you get up." Although asked like a question, the Old Woman, as Chie called her to herself, never asked questions.

Born before the war, like most people of her generation, the older woman was barely one and a half meters tall, but her sturdy body and strength belied her age. Sometimes.

"Your mother never said you were such a lazy girl. How can you just laze around when you know very well there is much to do."

"Yes, Mother," Chie said.

Now in the kitchen, Chie dipped the ladle into the dashi, fish and kelp broth, mixing it carefully with miso. She ladled a small amount into a bowl to taste if it had enough flavor. It was always just right.

"I thought you'd be a good worker, but you seem intent on proving yourself the laziest girl in the village," her mother-in-law went on as Chie placed the hot soup in front of her with two hands. Chie then handed her a bowl of rice, piled to the top the way she liked it. Although considered polite to serve a small amount at a time, the Old Woman was in no way genteel and told Chie when she moved in, "I don't want to have to ask twice for my rice. Give it to me at once."

"What would your mother think," she went on, swallowing whole her *tsukemono*, salted pickles, as she gulped down rice and washed it down with hot miso soup and tea. She wasn't in a hurry—that's just how she ate.

"Yes, Mother," Chie said. "I'm sorry."

Chie never liked calling her mother-in-law "Mother," but it was required. She was Chie's *giri no haha*—literally, the mother to whom one is obligated. Calling her Mother was respectful, polite, and expected. Chie couldn't call her anything else.

· · ·

Chie and the Old Woman took care of the fields. The family had stopped growing rice years earlier but kept tea fields, and a large section was reserved for vegetables, much more than they needed. The Old Woman kept Chie busy pickling everything and cutting thin strips of daikon to make the dried *kiriboshidaikon* they'd eat throughout the cooler months. Whole plots were left to flower and go to seed, and then the process started over again.

"Who will look after the fields when I'm gone if you don't become more determined." Another question that was not asked. Her monologue hardly varied from day to day, year to year.

Takashi continued to work at the subcontractor in town. It was monotonous, uninteresting work, and the pay poor, but he preferred it to the fields. He'd never worked at farming and never would.

"It looks like you'll never have children." The Old Woman had said that after they were married just a few months.

No. She never would, Chie thought. At the Old Woman's insistence, she'd been examined by a doctor. Although slim and with hips no wider than an adolescent boy's, she'd been assured she could have children. Chie remembered once reading that women who marry royalty must always submit to this kind of examination. She sensed what must be the loss of dignity for these women who wore hats and gloves and carried small pocketbooks, to have a doctor probing and poking. The book said that if the woman were a queen, no one was ever supposed to touch them, which led Chie to conclude the royal gynecologist must be given a special waiver so he or she can put their head and hands between the legs of these women who must prove they can bear kings.

No. She would never have children. She was certain. She wanted to tell the Old Woman, to put her mind at ease, but it would be considered impertinent. Although Takashi climbed on her with regularity, she knew from the beginning she would not make children.

Chie ate on in silence.

"Morning." It was her husband.

"Good morning." Chie answered, looked up, and stood up, all at once. She went to the kitchen to grill his fish. He ate fish every morning.

"Here," his mother said, rising. "Sit here." She took the seat adjacent to him that faced the kitchen and moved the dish of pickles closer to her son.

Chie came back in, poured his tea, and went back to the kitchen to turn the fish. Now the house, which had smelled of a freshly washed morning, had the smokey acrid smell of salted grilled fish. The tail, burned a crisp black, fell off as Chie took the fish off the grill. A light pall of smoke hung like a drop ceiling in the dark farmhouse kitchen.

Placing a rectangular dish of fish in front of him and placing the chopsticks at his right hand, she said, "It's going to be a nice day," and sat down again.

"Is this the ayu I caught?"

"No. My brother brought this over. We finished the other." Though she had said "we," Chie had never eaten fish in her life. She'd never been able to stand the smell.

"Get me some more shoyu, will you?"

"Oh, sorry." Chie rose to get the soy sauce.

Takashi wasn't demanding. It just would never have occurred to him to serve himself. He'd been waited on all his life. It was not an expectation, but his reality. If Chie had said

"Why don't you get it yourself?" he probably would have answered, "Oh sure," but his mother would have dropped dead on the spot. His mother regularly complained her son was not well taken care of by his wife, although he was literally waited on hand and foot. Chie handed him his lunch on his way out the door, arranged his shoes when he reentered the house.

Her own mother had died, but even if she'd been living, Chie would never have told her what it had been like once she entered her husband's household. The Old Woman not only lied about her, but concocted stories about events that had never happened—stories that turned up as gossip in the village. Any opportunity to humiliate and accuse Chie, in front of other family members, was never missed. She'd say the ofuro, the nightly bath, was too hot, or not hot enough. Scratches on a lacquer dish, a cracked teapot, a moth-eaten kimono, weevils in the rice bin, an inevitability in the old farmhouse—all were blamed on Chie.

It wasn't as if the Old Woman even meant to be mean. It was her right. She didn't know any other way to be. Chie's household situation was both typical and traditional. She was expected to do all the cooking, and it was equally expected her mother-in-law would complain: this dish is too sweet, that one too salty, and the *aji*, flavor, was not as good as her own. Making demands and being bossy was a mother-in-law's vocation. The Old Woman no doubt remembered her own experience of being the *o-yome-san*—bride, wife, daughter-in-law. Chie's mother-in-law bullied her seemingly as a pastime, as she herself must have been subjected to *yomeibiri*, bullying of a young wife. And whether it was about raising children they didn't have, or cooking, she freely gave her opinions and unsolicited advice. Although she often interfered in the young couple's personal lives, Chie could not expect her husband's backing, as he either didn't notice or, if he did, would blindly take his mother's side. Chie made no attempt to show her life as it was, but rather appeared as bright as her lovingly tended flower garden. She expertly hid her misery behind an easygoing temperament, a pleasant smile, and the carefully arranged fresh flowers in the entranceway.

Chie ate half a bowl of rice and drank a cup of tea. She was full. When her mother-in-law said, "Hurry now. I want to get started while it's still cool," she answered, "Yes, Mother." She was ready.

After making her husband's lunch and quickly washing up the breakfast things, hanging the laundry, and airing the bedding, Chie went to the back entranceway where the various things needed for the fields were kept. She slipped her feet into *jika-tabi*, the split-toe canvas work shoes, and then pulled on a smock. The smock had belonged to her mother, and the loose garment hung over her body like a tent. She tied her cotton bonnet under her chin, took her work gloves off the shelf. The Old Woman had chided her for using gloves. "The sooner your hands get tough, the better." The Old Woman's hands were like hide. Brown and hard, the calloused palms fit right into the grooved handles of the tools and didn't react to the ice-cold water of winter or to heat. Grabbing a sweet potato from hot coals, she'd pronounced on one occasion, "It's cooked enough." Chie had tried working without gloves, but her hands never grew calloused. They just got red and sore. The nails split unevenly across the tips, and the hard remnants dug into the soft flesh of her fingertips. *The tips of your fingers have more nerves than any other part of the body*, the science teacher had said. Chie didn't know why she continued to remember this lesson from years earlier when she had forgotten everything else. It didn't matter. She was in constant pain.

Hanging next to the tools on the wall was a large calendar, the days clearly marked with large black numbers, red numbers for holidays. Small characters written under the numbers showed if it was Taian, a good luck day. Chie never knew if it was a good luck day or not because she never wore her glasses. Each morning, her mother-in-law made a large cross through the day before. This day, a black-number day, wasn't marked yet.

She took the tools she needed down from the hooks: a small pitchfork, a short-handle scythe. She dipped the sharpening stone into the bucket of water that stood by the open door and moved the scythe's blade in even motions, back and forth, over the smooth stone. "Do it slowly and evenly if you want a good cutting edge," her mother-in-law had said. Chie thought it was the only useful instruction she'd had from her.

She walked on the short stone path that led away from the farmhouse. Down in the fields she could see just the top of her mother-in-law's bonnet, bobbing along among the low tea bushes. The Old Woman would do the east side today, Chie the west.

Chie stooped down among the bushes, and as if she'd gone there for that purpose, she took the curved blade of the scythe and guided it in a straight line across her left wrist. A clean cut. She was surprised how fast and steadily the blood ran out of her thin arm. Her mother's smock was now soaked with blood. She felt hot. Hot. It was a hot day. She pushed the cloth bonnet she'd just tied so neatly back on her head, leaving a perfect red handprint on the wide brim. She stretched out on her back, close to the tea bushes. She could see single raindrops still glistening clinging to vividly green tea leaves. The damp ground cooled her back and legs. Now she didn't feel hot but felt the comfortable warmth she always felt when she woke early, before everything began. Lying on her back she saw only blue sky. It was perfectly clear.

And no one would have thought the sun would come out that day.

END

ACKNOWLEDGEMENTS

It is my pleasure to first acknowledge novelist, memoirist, essayist, and theater director Roger Pulvers. I've admired him from afar for years for his many talents, extraordinary creative output, and most especially for his translations of Japanese literature. In recent years it has been my good fortune to have his encouragement and enjoy his humor and friendship.

I was fortunate indeed to work with the remarkable and redoubtable editor Toni Weeks. I was happy to have her guidance during the editing process, and I am grateful for the expertise she brought to this project.

For their generosity in making themselves available to read an early version of the manuscript, I am grateful to:
Sachiko Aoki, Kathleen Morikawa, Susan Ritz, and Beth Sakanishi. Literary ladies one and all, their individual insights and good sense were invaluable to me in the completion of this work.

Kathryn Guare is a "sherpa" to independent authors, and I am thankful for her time and skill in the production of this book. Thank you, Jennifer Taylor, for being my intrepid proofreader.

I was privileged to have Emily Mahon, who designed the cover of my memoir, again lend her creative talents to envision and design the cover of my novel.

It has been a joy to be a student of Osami Masuda (Japanese calligraphy), Hiroko Narushima (Hula) and William Spilka (Art History). My life has been enriched immeasurably by their passion for their subjects, which has been shared with great warmth.

I love to collaborate, and I thank Adam Fulford, Alec McAulay, Tom Pedersen, John Rucynski, Joseph Shaules, and Glen Wood for giving me the opportunity and pleasure to collaborate with them on various projects.

Among my contemporaries, I celebrate these writers for their talents and accomplishments:

Rachel Caldecott, Tamar Cole, Sarah Coomber, Rebecca Copeland, Kaori Fujimoto, Lise Funderburg, Alice Gordenker, Linda Gould, Suzanne Kamata, Jeffrey Kingston, Todd Jay Leonard, Edward Levinson, Leza Lowitz, Leanne Martin, Don McLaren, Jeffrey Miller, Kit Nagamura, Diane Nagatomo, Caroline Pover, Michael Pronko, Mark Schilling, Frederik Schodt, Ann Tashi Slater, Zakia Spalter, Louis Spaventa, Bob Tobin.

While I may never be able to express my gratitude to all those to whom I am grateful, please know your kind words and support have meant the world to me. Here, with great appreciation for their individual talents, I thank and acknowledge the generosity and friendship of many:

Gretchen Cook Anderson, Kathleen Aoki, Lilka and Tom Areton, Edward Balke, Bruce Batten, Jon Bauer, Madalina Bistriceanu, Dorian Benkoil, Cathy Bernatt, Teresa Blair, Thomas Boardman, Bhikkhu Bodhi, Solveig Boergen, Christine M. Brown, Matt Burney, Patricia Carlin, Regina Cronin, Sangita Rajbongshi Das, Sophie Dornstreich, Danielle DuBois Flax, Shohei Fukuda, Sarah Everitt Furuya, Emma Fushimi, Melissa Goldstein, Liubov Golubovskaya, Andrew Hankinson, Alison Harada, Takayo Harriman, Mieko Hikosaka, Satoko Hirakawa, Judith Hope, Nina Fallenbaum Ichikawa, Laura Inoue, Kiyoko Izuka, Bridgitte Jackson-Buckley, Leonard Jacobs, Joy Jarman-Walsh, Ann Jenkins, Rhonda Y.C. Johnson, Eric Johnston, Nura Kamar, Louise George Kittaka, Jeff Kreuger, Susana Kumagai, Linda Laddin, Isabelle Laskin, Peter Matanle, Austin Moore, Mayumi Motojima, Kristin Newton, Catherine O'Connell, Motoyo Okuwa, Benjamin Parks, Janet Pocorobba, Suzanne Price, Stephanie Prince, Angela Reynolds, Lynne Riggs, Melissa Rinne, Phil Robertson, Michael Rost, Louise Rouse, Noriko Sato, Eiko Shimizu, Jennifer Shinkai, Winifred Lewis Shiraishi, Ian Spalter, Agustin Spinetto, Anna Sumilat,William Swinton, Masami Takai, Ginny Tapley Takemori, Kazufumi Takeuchi, Karen Lee Tawarayama, Zen Tsujimoto, Helene Uchida, Geri Urquidez, Donna Vello, Nicole Watanabe, Robert Yellin.

Nanao, Mie, Mario, Lila:
You are the light of my life. You inspire me, and every day I am thankful I am your Mama.

Thank you, Billy, for the music and dancing, the caring, laughter and love, with which you've filled our life together.

ABOUT THE AUTHOR

Karen Hill Anton wrote the columns "Crossing Cultures" for the *Japan Times* and "Another Look" for the Japanese newspaper *Chunichi Shimbun* for fifteen years. Her essays, articles, and other writing have appeared in collections, publications, and textbooks in Japan and abroad. She lectures internationally on her experience of cross-cultural adaptation, and raising four bilingual, bicultural children. Karen is the author of the widely acclaimed memoir *The View From Breast Pocket Mountain*, Grand Prize Winner of the 2022 Memoir Prize for Books, 2021 B.R.A.G Medallion, and the 2020 SPR Book Awards Gold Prize. Originally from New York City, she has made her home with her husband William Anton in the rural province of Shizuoka, Japan, since 1975.

KarenHillAnton.com

Milton Keynes UK
Ingram Content Group UK Ltd.
UKHW041157160923
428809UK00001B/1

9 798218 109844